Ezekiel's Wheels

F. M. PHILLIPS

Cover art and graphic design by Murv Jacob.

This is a work of fiction. Names, characters, places, and incidents either are the product of the author's imagination or are used fictitiously. Any resemblance to actual persons, living or dead, events, or locales is entirely coincidental.

EZEKIEL'S WHEELS. Copyright © 2013 by F.M. Phillips. All rights reserved. Printed in the United States of America.

No parts of this book may be used or reproduced in any manner whatsoever without written permission, except in the case of brief quotations embodied in critical articles and reviews. For more information, contact F.M. Phillips at fthphillips@gmail.com.

All rights reserved.

ISBN-10: 1480132357

ISBN-13: 9781480132351

Grateful acknowledgment is made to reprint the following song lyric excerpts:

How Long, written by Paul Carrack, performed by Ace
Chain of Fools, written by Don Covay, performed by Aretha Franklin
Everybody's Talkin', written and performed by Harry Nilsson
Riders on the Storm, written by Jim Morrison, performed by The Doors
Little Hideaway, written and performed by Leon Russell
Moving In Stereo, written by Ric Ocasek and Greg Hawkes, performed by The Cars
What's Goin' On, written by Renaldo "Obie" Benson, Al Cleveland, and Marvin Gaye, performed by Marvin Gaye
Lady Blue, written and performed by Leon Russell
Ashes to Ashes, written and performed by David Bowie
House of the Rising Sun, Unknown Author, arrangement by Dave Van Ronk, performed by The Animals
A Thousand Miles From Nowhere, written and performed by Dwight Yoakum
I'm On Fire, written and performed by Bruce Springsteen
Don't Cry, written by Izzy Stradlin and Axl Rose, performed by Guns N' Roses
Sara, written by Stevie Nicks, performed by Fleetwood Mac
This Masquerade, written and performed by Leon Russell
Golden Bird, written by Happy Traum, performed by Levon Helm

Acknowledgments

To Steve Ripley, the Mad Scientist of Oklahoma Rock and Roll, and his inestimable wife, Charlene Ripley. Without the influence of your peerless radio program, this story would have never materialized.

For all The Ones who believed and knew none of it was a coincidence.

Love to my technical advisor, LDF, for his expert advice on gasoline, flash fires, slip joint pliers, and dental work.

Special acknowledgment and love always to my Little Bear and original editor-in-chief, JCDS.

For the memory of loved ones already gone away from this place—we will meet you on the shore.

Chapter 1

Shell

> *But there ain't any use in pretending, it could happen to us any day.* Ace, "How Long"

"In England they call it a will-o'-the-wisp," she said, folding a pair of underwear into thirds.

Leonard poked his head out from behind the bathroom door. His wiry eyebrows inched together and two vertical lines formed at the center of his forehead, in the universal expression of puzzlement. The sight of him was a comical one, though she did not laugh. His head appeared to have detached, and levitated on its own in the lingering hot shower fog.

"Say what, babe?"

"The Spooklights, I mean. They've been sighted all over the world. Almost every culture has a name for them. Southerners call them ghost lights. The Brits say will-o'-the-wisp. Ignis Fatuus."

"Ah. Right." His tone fell flat and hollow, then, with disinterest. His head disappeared back into the bathroom and he busied himself with a quick shave. The dull razor blade scraped coarse black hairs off his chin. *Whssk, whsssk.*

"You know you don't have to go this weekend if you don't want to," she said. "I won't mind making the drive on my own. Not one bit. Fact, it might do us some good to spend a little time apart." She hesitated, perched on the bed amidst a light-colored mound of washed laundry. She tilted her head in the direction of the bathroom, anticipating his reply.

Len emerged in the bedroom with a small towel wrapped around his waist. A light steam rose off his back and its wispy tendrils reached up to the ceiling and vanished into the cool air of the bedroom.

"Do us good? What is *that* supposed to mean?" he demanded. "I *want* to go. I couldn't give two shits about the goblin light or whatever you like to call it. But I do like the idea of a road trip, and anyway I don't want to stay here all weekend on my own."

Shell looked up again and flashed a forced smile. She said no more and picked up a collared dress shirt from the laundry pile. She whipped its creases out into the air. Her outstretched arms slung the material with a little more force than usual.

Since Leonard had officially announced his intention to make the trip, she knew her weekend plans must be altered. A two-night stay with her parents was now out of the question. They would do well to make it through twelve hours at her family's home without some sort of awkward scene. Leonard tended to speak his mind without the help of a filter for appropriateness. Words that materialized in his brain in a given moment were destined to tumble unchecked, right on out of his mouth, regardless of present company. He much favored curse words to the commonplace language of proper folk and took great pride in setting them out on display in lengthy strings of profanity. Shell pled for discretion, and Leonard would promise it in return, but given an audience of at least one, the man felt compelled to entertain–and his promises would quickly de-materialize as if they'd never existed in the first place, spirited away and forgotten. His raucous demeanor held the attention of most at the beginning of his rants, but by the time he was finished, the great majority found themselves put out and offended. Their horrified reactions were indeed Leonard's great delight.

Leonard's flippant disregard for social constraints was one of the first attributes Shell found herself drawn to when they first met. But, as so often happens in relationships, his initial charms were now uncomfortable liabilities. She no longer looked forward to accompanying him in public, and dreaded the few awkward appearances he made around her family back home. It was just as well because Len harbored a strong aversion to time spent with the Fosters, and with any other family in general. The inclination came naturally; he had never been particularly close to his own.

Shell had planned the weekend trip as a release valve of sorts—a temporary Band-Aid for her increased frustration with Leonard, and a short little weekend jaunt to escape the stress. Just for a day or two, kill two birds and all. Said and done, the road trip figured to be a solid twelve-hour drive. Len hated long drives. Her hope that he would take a pass on the weekend was not all that unreasonable.

Shell made a quick mental run of the directions she had mapped out for the drive. She failed to notice Len step across the cream-colored carpet between the bathroom and the bedside. He stuck his hand inside the top of the small towel wrapped around his waist. In one smooth motion, he pulled out the corner tucked in at the top, and dropped the towel to the carpet in a damp heap of thread.

"Look at me babe. Look at this. All of *this* is yours," he said in grand pronouncement. He lifted his arms as he spoke, one palm facing the ceiling while the other gestured down at his leafless form.

She looked up from her laundry once again and expected to find that Len was joking. She saw from his solemn expression that he was not joking at all. To her dismay, he appeared quite serious.

The chemistry between them had suffered for months. Their relationship was treading water at best, and on the verge of going under. Her libido had stopped paddling months before. At his continued behest, she gave in and glanced over to make an honest evaluation. Her eyes had laid sight of his form hundreds of times before, and she was certain now that nothing short of a miracle could rekindle her interest.

But there would be no miracle. It occurred to her that Len resembled a sinewy vine, shriveled dry in the dead heat of a summer drought. He was steel-rail skinny and his biceps rivaled her own in their lack of definition. He stood at exactly six feet tall and didn't weigh more than a buck sixty, sopping wet.

Shell's eyes hastened away from Len's emaciated trunk and darted upward to his taut face. A broad smile displayed gums that would have better complimented a larger set of teeth. At last her gaze settled on his lively brown eyes. Len looked down at her in earnest. She was grateful he could not read her mind. Despite her increased apathy she felt no desire to hurt his feelings.

"How about it, babe? A quick one before we leave? You won't be in the mood if we stay at your parents' house tonight. It *has* been over a week, you know. Just let me do all the work."

"We don't have time, Len!" she said, and hoped he would relent.

"Come on, I've got something for you," he said. He reached his hand out toward her and Shell involuntarily angled her body away in the opposite direction. But he continued to reach past and picked something up from the bedside table. It was her iPod.

"Look here, I made a play list for you. Something for us to listen to on the road trip."

Leonard's typical music selections consisted in large part of euro trash and pop from the early '90s, so Shell appraised this list with a suspicious eye. But this time she was surprised to see a handful of old favorites.

"Where did you come up with these songs, Len?" she asked, amused.

"I just went through the iPod and picked the ones I liked," he said with a sly, sarcastic smile.

"Mmhmm. So, you've been a closet Leon Russell fan all this time? Funny you never mentioned that before."

"Okay, okay, fine. I just looked through your 'Favorites' list yesterday and some of them caught my eye."

The corner of Shell's mouth turned up in a crooked smile, and she decided to give him a break. It was the equivalent of a mixtape, and a gesture of affection, as far as she was concerned.

"You know what? That was pretty sweet of you, Len. I can't wait to hear it. We'll turn it on the minute we get on the road. Now help me finish up with this laundry so we can get packed and get out of here."

Len hesitated for a moment. His hopes, among other things, were raised since he stepped out of the hot shower. Still, he knew the chances of changing Shell's mood were not good.

"Okay. Let's get this show on the road. But you'll owe me one later." He tousled her chestnut hair, went to the closet, and pulled out a black duffel bag and a suitcase.

After they finished packing, Len shouldered the luggage and lurched toward the front door. His weekend necessities, in their entirety, fit snugly into a single duffel bag. Shell's suitcase, on the other hand, strained at the seams. Len squeezed through the front door after some effort and a few mumbled words regarding women and packing.

Shell remained inside, checking to make sure she hadn't forgotten anything. She combed through her purse to be certain it was all there. The camera was a must, plus car chargers, her laptop, car keys, and sunglasses. Now she was ready.

As she walked down the hallway toward the front door, hands overrun with keys and electronics, she sensed a slight change in the air. She was struck by the unmistakable sensation that some presence besides her own was in the room.

"Len?" She asked aloud, though she knew he was already outside at the car.

A whoosh of air pushed a strand of hair back from her face. Something dark flew past her cheek. Startled, she ducked low and took in a quick, shallow breath. Crouched in the floor, she looked back over her shoulder. She barely made out a tiny dark figure at the end of the hall, just before it flew into her bedroom.

Footsteps sounded in the entryway. Len strode into the hall to find Shell still crouched on the floor.

"What the hell?"

"Something just flew down the hall!" She exclaimed. "I couldn't see what it was, but it flew right past me into the bedroom!"

"What was it?" He asked.

"I just told you, I don't know. I didn't even see where it came from."

Len sidestepped Shell, grabbed the handle to the bedroom door, and slammed it shut.

"What the hell was it?" He asked again and turned to face Shell. "If you're playing a game with me, Shell—If you're trying to scare me before we go on this childish little ghost hunt of yours, I don't think it's funny. We're already short on time as it is."

Shell found herself amused at the level of alarm in Leonard's voice. He was frightened. She stood and walked to the end of the hall.

"Move, Len."

She opened the white cabinet door on the wall behind him and pulled out a tan bed sheet.

"What's your big plan with that?" He asked.

Shell noted the mocking tone in his voice and gave no reply. She opened the bedroom door, slipped inside and pushed it closed behind her. She could still hear Len's muffled voice. He continued to ramble on from the other side of the door.

She stood alert and quiet. Her pupils dilated in the darkened room. Without looking, she reached behind her back and flipped the wall switch to turn on the lighted ceiling fan. Her eyes darted from one corner to the next, watching for movement. She suddenly regretted not tidying the room after they packed. Stacks of folded laundry sat atop the comforter and vanity chair. Len's wet towel lay in the same spot of carpet where he'd dropped it. An empty gym bag was unzipped on the floor.

Plenty of places to hide in here, she thought to herself. She turned to her left and eyed the closet. The light bulb had burned out just the day before. *I bet it's in the closet, where it's dark.*

Shell raised the sheet until it was just under her chin. She took slow, measured steps toward the closet while her mind tripped over itself in a hurried attempt to marry what she saw in the hall with any measure of reason.

With a full-on posture she faced the closet, reached out and pushed a handful of hangers out of the way. The metal hooks screeched down the pole. At once, a frantic scratching sound erupted from behind her. She wheeled around and knew immediately where the *thing*, whatever it was, had taken refuge. It was underneath the bed, at the very back by the headboard. Another scratch sounded against the wall. Three loud raps came with great force against the door. Shell jumped, her nerves balanced on a razor's edge.

"Damn it, Shell. What are you doing in there?"

She continued to ignore Len and walked to the headboard, where she dropped down on her knees. Very slowly, she reached out and lifted the red satin coverlet that covered the empty space from the bed frame to the floor. She bent at the waist and craned her neck sideways for a look, hoping that the distance was enough to block whatever it was, if the thing tried to make an escape. But in the darkness under the bed she couldn't make out anything at all. Past a couple of inches, it was complete blackness under there.

She stood and hurried back to the door and eased it open just a crack.

"I need my cell phone, Len," she whispered.

"Who are you calling?" He asked. The frantic scratching resumed at the sound of his voice.

"Be quiet," she said in a hushed voice. "Please. Just get me the phone."

Len fetched the phone for her, and Shell shut the door again. She walked back over to the bed and once again lifted the red coverlet. She pressed the number three on the phone's keypad and the green screen illuminated a small area of the floor. A flurry of movement erupted just as the light pierced the darkness. A pair of wings burst straight out at her face. She screamed a short, muted cry and fell backward onto her haunches on the floor.

Shell tilted her head back and followed the flight of the menace across the short distance to the bathroom. It came to rest on the antique light fixture above her sink, its beak agape, its eyes as terrified as her own. It was only a bird. A little barn swallow.

"You moron," she whispered to herself, "What did you *think* it was?"

She pushed herself up from the floor and stepped into the bathroom. When she was close enough, she flung the bed sheet atop the light fixture and the bird was captured. After a few seconds of frantic winged melee, the bird went still and Shell folded the edges of the sheet underneath. She picked up the bundle and walked out of the bedroom, down the hall, and out the front door.

Once outside, Shell eased to the ground, legs folded beneath her. She found a level place in the yard and set the little bundle of bird and blanket there. She feared she might break the swallow's wing, so with gentle hands she lifted the folds of the sheet one by one and pulled them away as though unwrapping a delicate birthday present. Once uncovered, the bird sat upright and perfectly still.

Shell leaned in closer for a better look. The bird's little eyes were like tiny vanilla beans, shiny and solid black. She saw in them a dark mirrored reflection of the outside world. The bird's head cocked to the side at a curious angle. It appeared to evaluate her in turn. She held her breath and reached out with care to try and stroke its feathers with her index finger.

"Sonofabitch, *SHELL!*"

Len flung open the screen door and it smashed against the red brick wall of the porch. In an instant, the swallow took to the air and flew from sight.

"Can you *please*, and I'm begging you here, *PLEASE*, stop playing Steve-Fucking-Irwin with that bird and get in the goddam car? Be nice to make it out of the city by midnight, wouldn't it?"

Shell stared after the swallow's flight and said, "I really don't want to go anymore."

Len's eyes widened and he shook his head from side to side in disgust. "Oh for fuck's sake. I just want to get on the road, Shell.

Please don't get started with the dramatics. I'm sorry for yelling. Let's just forget about all this and leave."

"My Grandma had a superstition about a bird in the house" she continued on, distracted, as though he'd never spoken. Her face was still turned up to the sky, eyes searching. "When we were kids, she told us that it meant someone close would die soon. A sign that death was near."

Len started to walk away but stopped short and returned to face Shell. He put a hand on either side of her face and slid his fingers through her dark hair to the back of her head. He gently pulled her line of sight back down from the sky to level with his.

"Don't you worry about that one, sweetheart," he said. "Because if you don't hop your happy ass into that car, I'll kill my *SELF*. Then Grandma will finally receive the credit she's due, and you two hysterics can live happily ever after with Tweety."

Shell did not want to smile. His sarcastic dismissal felt like a pinprick of humiliation to her ego. Then again, she did feel pretty silly for talking about an old superstition from so long ago. She considered the entire scene a second time, then tilted her head back and laughed. What a ridiculous sight she must have been, running through the house with a sheet over her head like a cuckoo clanswoman. It was really no wonder he made fun.

Leonard at first found himself confused and taken aback by her laughter. She had been so defensive and on edge the past few months. A good many more harsh words than usual had been exchanged between them. This time, though, he felt a great wash of relief at the sound of her laughter. He began to laugh along too and decided it was a sign that their awkward tension might at last make its final retreat. He thought perhaps the weekend trip might be their best chance to finally get things back to normal.

The ill mood of the bird's bad omen was broken. Shell returned to the house to gather her things without another word of protest. *Len is right*, she thought. *It's time to get on the road.*

Chapter 2

Shell

> *You told me to leave you alone,*
> *my father said come on home.*
> Aretha Franklin, "Chain of Fools"

Shell was excited to see her sister again. The Foster girls were separated in age by less than a year, yet they adhered with no effort at all to the personality traits set out in most birth order studies. Shell was independent, driven, and ambitious. She considered herself capable and responsible. Jennifer was the baby of the family, in need of a steady diet of attention, and was a determined irritant if she didn't receive her fair share. While Shell felt most thoughts were best served in silence, Jennifer believed hers wasted unless broadcast for all who would listen.

By outward appearances, strangers would never pair the two together as sisters. Shell was dark-haired with the rich olive-smooth skin of their mother's Cherokee ancestry. Jennifer's countenance borrowed from the traits of the Foster line. She was born with comical tufts of white-blonde hair, near-transparent white skin and blue eyes.

Despite their differences, the girls held each other in high regard and only on rare occasions reached the point of argument. The few times they did become cross, Jenny would find herself castigated and sent from the room in frustration. On occasion, Shell became aggravated with her sister to the point of physical retaliation, but even then she could never quite bring herself to inflict real bodily harm. During the worst of Jennifer's tantrums, the most effective response Shell summoned was a weak-willed episode of hair pulling that embarrassed them both. Shell's method served as a means of keeping Jennifer at arm's length until their mother arrived to intercede. Even after the occasional power struggle, they would part ways satisfied that justice had been served–Jennifer with her bit of calculated attention, and Shell with solitude restored. Neither would have guessed that in future years they would become the closest of confidantes.

After Shell left for college, Jennifer stayed behind ostensibly to remain close to their parents. She felt obliged to care for them even though they remained in fine health. In truth, Jennifer was the one who sought to be looked after. Shell, on the other hand, was not encumbered by any sense of obligation and enjoyed the dangerous, liberated sensation of cart-wheeling through her twenties without the immediate weighty influence of familial roots. There was a sense of relief when she returned home to see the family because she missed them terribly. But there was an equal amount of joy in the high-flying freedom that came when it was once again time to leave. She felt a sense of importance and self-worth, with the certain knowledge that hers was a dire responsibility to make a success of her own life, and she relished the knowledge that she bore this responsibility alone.

She had declared to her family at the tender age of ten that she had no intention whatsoever of marrying or having children. It was a strange pronouncement for a young girl in rural Oklahoma, where marrying young was both expected and often encouraged.

But her parents agreed and encouraged her pursuits. No one was surprised when she followed through and announced plans to leave for college to become a nurse. The Fosters were dismayed when she chose to make her residence with Leonard in Oklahoma City after graduation, but they knew she was compelled by some inner combustion to conduct life on her own terms, and because of that the family felt proud and held her in a respectful, if not slightly bewildered, regard.

Shell Foster grew up caring little for the company of other girls. She held a strong prejudice against her peers, based on unfair, broad generalizations of girlish rainbow ponies and tiny doll houses in which other girls her age replicated the boring preoccupations of household duties. Their hobbies and conversations bored her to the very limit of her tolerance, so she avoided them and sought out the company of adults. She preferred heated political debates, rich with discussion of war and the tedious balances of power. Her father happened upon her one Sunday morning as she sat all by herself with breakfast, engaged by the musings of William F. Buckley, Jr. in a stolid appearance on a news program. At that age she had no real concept of the nations or people that held court in these conversations, but she nonetheless reveled in the seriousness with which they were conducted. Afterward, she would go to her room and examine her globe, a most treasured possession, to scour the planet for the names of the exotic lands mentioned. In her active imagination, she pictured a great war on the horizon, the likes of which she conceived of as vast wastelands of nuclear fallout, all of them derived from apocalyptic war movies popular in the 1980s. She imagined herself a tough underground subversive, lobbing grenades at unmanned flying machines and frantically directing the poor mutt bastards that had managed to survive a nuclear winter into a fine machination of a fighting force.

Jennifer Foster was flummoxed as to the reason her sister was entertained by subjects so repulsively bland and masculine. She herself was already concerned with earning the attention of the boys at school, and spent large blocks of time at the mirror in the morning, carefully arranging her hair just so. She maintained a fresh coat of matching paint on her fingernails and toes at all times, and kept a tube of lip gloss at the ready in case an emergency need rose for reapplication. Their personalities developed alongside one another, a yin and yang on their own natural arcs through adolescence and high school.

One day Jennifer asked Shell about her philosophy on aging: "So what do you think will happen when we get to be middle-aged? When we start to get wrinkles. Like when we're in our thirties?"

Shell was confused. "What do you mean?" She asked, annoyed to require clarification from her little sister.

"Don't you think you'll want plastic surgery?" she asked.

"Why would I?" Shell replied.

"God, you don't want to look like that, do you?" Jenny said and gestured at the civics teacher who had just sat down for lunch at the nearby teachers' table. She was busy unpacking her food from a brown paper bag, setting each item out in a straight line, blissfully unaware of the impromptu evaluation by two young girls. Shell noted that Mrs. Carter did indeed appear quite pained by time. The top layer of her skin was sallow and hung in folds here and there like semi-transparent pieces of crepe paper.

"First of all, Jennifer, Mrs. Carter is not in her thirties. She's much older than that," Shell offered. "And secondly, I'd rather be like her than some of the sad actors in the movies who look like their faces have been sucked up by a giant vacuum."

They both had a good laugh, and Shell continued on: "If I'm lucky enough to live as long as Mrs. Carter, I hope I have even *more* wrinkles than she does."

Jennifer rolled her eyes and waited for the rest. Shell was setting up another of her grand revelations that often proved novel, and at times impressive in scope. Even the musings that turned out to be pure imaginary piles of horse shit at least served to entertain. Shell appreciated the opportunity likewise, because as the younger Foster, Jennifer had no choice but to fill the role of captive audience.

Shell obliged the encouragement of her sister's raised eyebrows and continued, "I just hope that someday people will look at me and see a life lived. Every line on my face will tell the story of a day on the river or a hike through the woods. Some struggle I lived through. Some barrier I fought my way over. You don't live a life like that and come away unscathed. A life lived well shows through in the face. So let some proper lady have porcelain skin at age seventy. When I see her I'll know that she sat sheltered in a darkened room and took care of her face—and I'm sure I'll admire her flawless skin; I just won't envy it. Because then I can go look in my own mirror and remember all of the sun and wind and games and trouble wrinkled at the corner of my eyes and across my forehead. My face will be lined just like a book. And I'll be proud of it."

Jennifer looked at her sister with a combination of contempt and admiration. A strange pair, but she felt them in equal parts for Shell. "You're so weird."

"So are you."

※ ※ ※

After Shell left for college, the dynamics of her relationship with Jennifer shifted dramatically. It was a slow and gradual change, not visible to the naked eye. Like the movement of a glacier perhaps: not actively perceived, but easily predicted. The day came when Jennifer was the full-grown version of her precocious younger self. She discovered that she enjoyed Shell's conversation even more so than she enjoyed the role of needy provocateur. With adulthood they became great friends. Shell came to feel the same regard for Jennifer too, though hers was a longer transition. In some ways, Jennifer must remain the pest of a younger sister. And Shell would always remain obliged to look after her. After twenty years they became like old friends, and all traces of rivalry simply faded away.

When the idea for the Spooklight endeavor came to Shell's mind, she very seriously considered asking Jennifer along. Her sister would have jumped at the chance to be the wingman on such a prodigious undertaking. She would have ribbed Shell without mercy at first, but then it would have been all green lights and checkered flags.

The Hornet Spooklight had been lost in the junk pile of Shell's subconscious memory for years, reemerging only a month before. Autumn had been rolling in on the front of a nasty, biting wind that blew in perpetual sheets of rain. Her weekend plans to work at cleaning up the little flower plot in the front yard were scrapped, and the storm outside provided a fine excuse to waste an entire afternoon on the couch. Armed with a collection of junk food and a blanket, she flipped through hundreds of dull channels on the TV guide until a title popped up and demanded attention.

The program was entitled *Mystery in the Ozarks,* and Shell clicked on it, eager to spot footage of the forests and hilly landscapes she remembered so fondly from childhood. She gathered from the dated cars and wardrobes that the show must be a re-run. The first segment was an embarrassment and featured a hulking, ill-spoken Cretan of a man called, of all things, Bubba, who trudged through the dense Ozark forests. He was a heavy mouth-breather who prattled on about the putrid smell on the wind that he knew, without question, to be the familiar whiff of the sasquatch.

Shell smiled to herself and remembered some of the old stories the kids back home repeated about so-and-so's aunt, who had come face to face with a red-eyed hairy beast that peered in through the kitchen window at night. *Probably one of their kin folk stumbled home from the bar,* Shell thought, amused.

Bubba was one of many predictable thorns in the side of most Okies. Anytime the state made national news because of tornado damage or some other dire event, reporters consistently sought out the most offensive of representatives among the population. It was always some hollow-cheeked tweaker who, sometimes in need of closed captioned translation, harped on about the inescapable wrath of God or some other meth-wheeled ramble.

The next segment caused Shell to betray her bag of Fritos for the moment. It was a special about a strange phenomenon found at the tri-state border called the Hornet Spooklight. The program interviewed a few locals eager to toss in their two cents about the light. One store owner in Wyandotte blamed headlights from the nearby interstate. Next was a man who said it was the wandering ghost of a headless miner killed in an accident at the Harden zinc mine back in the '20s. He flashed a mouthful of gums at the end of his story, staring sober into the camera to deliver his punch line: "And on quiet nights they can still hear Headless Bill, wandering through the hills, moaning and hollering, 'Who chopped my top ... *WHO CHOPPED MY TOP?*'" With this, he threw his head back and cackled like a loon.

The last interview of the segment was with a rather serious-looking dark-skinned man of advanced age, who told the tragic local legend of a young Cherokee couple who killed themselves in despair. He claimed the Native Americans in the area believed the light to be the unsettled spirits of the two lovers, bound in eternity to haunt the location of their desperate end.

Video footage of the area showed a hand-hewn wooden sign that pointed rather unobtrusively down a gravel road in the direction of "Devil's Promenade." The cameraman provided viewers with a first-hand point of view over the edge of a rocky precipice that jutted out at least two hundred feet above the Illinois River. The banks below were lined with giant, hulking boulders that must have shifted down the hillside over the course of hundreds of years. They stood like a haphazard line of nature's sentries, guarding the river's southern boundary.

When the fifteen-minute segment reached its end, Shell stared at the television while a cheery voice reminded her that "choosy moms choose Jiff." She paid no mind to the commercials. Her mind was at work filtering through the old mental file storage at the farthest reaches of her memory.

Where did I hear that story before? she wondered. It was that last story, the one about the Cherokee couple, that invoked an uncanny sense of déjà vu. After nearly an entire minute of staring blankly ahead, her chin lifted and she snapped her fingers in the air. The Hornet Spooklight was a story she and her sister heard for the first time when they were just girls.

During those days the two little Foster girls found nothing more delicious on a summer evening than an adventure down on the river. Their nights were filled with tales of great black panthers, lumbering Sasquatch and strange glowing lights in the sky.

The stories their father told might as well have been the gospel truth. Shell and Jennifer became transfixed from the first word, listening rapt and pie-eyed, their mouths agape.

Whether or not any of the old legends were true never mattered to the girls at all. They were at once terrified and enamored with the notion that secretive creatures stalked the dark woods and haunted the night skies around their home.

Of all the supernatural lore nestled deep in Shell's mind, the story of the Spooklight intrigued her most. Her father began the story one evening while she and her little sister sat on the rocky gravel bed of the river bank, roasting marshmallows over a fire. With a warm beer in one hand, and a Marlboro Red in the other, Dean Foster leaned forward in his seat and pushed up the bill of his cap. The reflection of the campfire danced in his eyes and gave him a mischievous, devil-may-care facade.

"You girls know the story of Romeo and Juliet, don't you?" He said this as a statement, rather than a question, because he already knew their answer. The sisters nodded in silent unity.

"Something a lot like that happened right around here a long time ago. During that time the tribal land of the Cherokees was located in Georgia. The people lived there for thousands of years. When the Europeans came, they set up a government. Most of the Cherokees accepted the changes because they wanted to live in peace with their families. The Cherokees wanted to keep their homeland. They settled down and developed an alphabet. They taught their children to read and write English, and even gave many of them English names."

"After they lived in peace among the whites for hundreds of years, someone discovered gold in the mountains of Georgia, and they found it right in the middle of the land that everyone, even the government, agreed belonged to the Cherokee people. But the government ordered the Cherokees to leave their homes. Thousands of families had to go; old people, even, and little babies. If they were Indian they had to leave. The military rounded them up and made them walk across the country to Oklahoma. Some of your great-great-great-*great* grandparents were Cherokees who walked all the way here from Georgia."

"The Trail of Tears!" Jennifer Foster interjected.

"Shut up, you moron!" Put out by the interruption, Shell jabbed her elbow into her sister's ribs as hard as she could. Jennifer cried out and dropped the end of her roasting stick into the fire. The marshmallow flamed and burned into a charred blob of molten sugar.

"Settle down, Shell, and go get another marshmallow for your sister. You're right, Jenny, it was the Trail of Tears."

Shell returned from the pickup truck with a marshmallow impaled half way down a new twig. Jennifer snatched it from her grasp and held her treat over the fire, roasting it with a grudge. Her eyes were narrowed with anger and she eyed Shell sideways through little slits. Shell ignored the dirty look and settled back in her seat.

Dean Foster began again, perturbed by the interruption. "Now listen, both of you. Sit still and listen. There was a Cherokee family with a beautiful daughter who was sixteen or so—just a little older than you girls are now.

"She was the only child in their family and her parents were very protective. Their journey led them near small towns all along the trail, but most of the people refused to allow the Cherokees to enter, even to buy supplies. The march began in October, and as the winter months came on the family nearly froze to death. Food was hard to find. They stopped outside a town in Kentucky and a young white man rode up on the camp. His name was Major.

"When Major found them in trouble, he rushed back to town and brought extra blankets and food for the family. They stayed there for a week while the family recovered, and every day Major rode out to bring food and water. In just those few days, he and the Cherokee girl fell in love—but they knew that they had to keep it a secret from her parents. Major and the girl made a secret vow to marry once the family reached their new home in Indian Territory. Major asked her to wait for him, and swore he would follow her and tell the family about their plans.

"Well, the family continued on their journey and made it across the border from Missouri into Oklahoma. The girl began to fear that Major might never come back, but he finally tracked them down. At first, the family welcomed him in, remembering his kindness. But when the daughter confessed her love for Major, and that she would marry him, her parents forbade the marriage and told Major that he must leave and never return.

"That night the Cherokee girl slipped away and met Major on a cliff overlooking the river. It was a full moon, just like tonight. The two decided they could not live without each other and jumped from the edge to their deaths on the rocks below.

"When they were discovered missing, the people formed search parties and went out looking for them. The girl's mother was the one who found her daughter. Even in death they still held hands. They never let go of each other, even during that long fall to the bottom of the cliff. Her parents were grief stricken and lived the rest of their lives with broken hearts." He paused, as though the story had reached its conclusion.

"Then what?" Shell demanded.

"They say that to this day, on a moonlit night, if you go to that cliff on the river, the spirits of those two young lovers will find you. They come out at dusk: a couple of glowing lights that float up and down the riverbed, searching for each other. The place where it happened isn't too far from here. Just a couple hours north. It's called Devils Promenade."

"Daddy! Will you take us to see the Spooklight?" Jennifer begged.

"Of course I will."

"What does the light do? Is it bad?" Shell asked. She was troubled by the story and could not make sense of the Cherokee girl's death.

"No one knows for sure. Most of the time people can't get up close to the lights. But I've heard tell that some people get chased by them. The Cherokees say the light can cause a man to lose his mind. In fact, most of the Indians stay away from that place altogether. They think it's bad medicine."

"I don't believe it," Shell said, baiting her father for more information.

"Scientists have traveled to Oklahoma from all around the world to study the Spooklight. The military sent a team down in the fifties to try and figure it out. After all these years, no one's ever explained it. Some of the scientists said it was just the headlights of cars passing by on the interstate."

"Is that what you think, Dad?"

"No, I don't think so, because stories about the light were here long before the interstate. A long time before cars, even. Maybe you'll just have to go see for yourself one day. What do you think about that?"

Shell opened her mouth to answer, but before she managed a word, a hoot owl called from the opposite creek bank. The night became very still except for the trinkling sound of the river over the rocks.

Jenny broke the silence: "Hey, Dad, can we go home now? I'm starting to get cold." Her thin arms were wrapped around her body, and she chattered her teeth for emphasis.

"Okie doke. Help me pack up camp, girls, and we'll head back to the hacienda. I'll bet your mom has some hot cocoa waiting for us on the stove anyway."

Shell rode shotgun on the ride home and bounced along on the bench seat of their Chevy pickup. She stared out the window, chin rested on fist, looking into the woods for any sign of strange floating lights. She hoped that none would appear.

After that night on the river, Shell remembered the Spooklight here and there, usually after all the lights went out at bedtime. On one or two occasions she brought the subject up to her father, but he never seemed too interested, and the discussion always turned to more salient matters. The legend of the Spooklight faded away with time and she moved on, from the mysteries that haunt the imaginations of children to the more pressing problems that occupy the minds of young women.

But then by chance, so many years later, Shell Foster was reminded of her youthful preoccupation by the happenstance of a rainy afternoon. The gears of fate made a decided shift in the direction of the Oklahoma/Missouri border. She began to design a plan that would at last satisfy the curiosity of her twelve-year-old psyche. A portentous journey of two days and many miles was set in motion.

Chapter 3

Rachel

> *People stopping, staring. I can't see their faces,
> only the shadows of their eyes.*
> Harry Nilsson, "Everybody's Talkin'"

Rachel Reese was busy tying the stems of black-eyed Susans around her wrist when the knocks sounded at the door. She paused and tilted her head in the direction of the hallway to try and overhear the hushed voices filtering through the air. In the front room her parents exchanged a grim knowing glance. They had been expecting unwelcome visitors for months now. Rachel's mother, Ani, gathered up a quilt and held it close against her chest for the simple comfort of occupied hands. She feared William might lose his composure and be taken away. His temper was fierce and if provoked he would not hesitate to fight the soldiers, rifles and all. He nodded in her direction and walked with his strong and steady gait to the door. Just outside, the group of soldiers stood at attention in smart blue uniforms. The blushed and flustered countenance of the man in front betrayed his young age. He could not have been more than a few years older than Rachel herself, but the uniform and rifle lent him an authoritative air.

"It is time for you to leave." The soldier spoke at a near-shout so everyone in the home would hear. "Bring your family and supplies. The contingent is gathering at the stockade."

"My family has not yet finished gathering our provisions," William said in a calm and reserved voice. "We face a journey of many months ahead. Will you allow us an hour more to prepare?"

The soldier hesitated and looked behind, as though he might find direction from his fellow soldiers.

"I have orders to get every Cherokee out and moved down to the stockade. We will return for you in a half-hour's time. Then you and your family will leave, either with your supplies or nothing at all."

The wooden porch groaned under the weight of the men as they turned and departed along the wagon-worn path that led through a grove of walnut trees and on to the other Cherokee settlements in New Echota.

William Reese shut the door and turned to face his family. Uncertainty was stamped across their drawn expressions.

"There is no time. We will leave behind everything that is not necessary to survive and we must move with speed. When the soldiers return we will be ready."

Not another word was spoken while the four set about gathering the last of their supplies. William had known this bitter day was at hand, and his family was prepared to the extent preparation was possible. Still, the hard realization landed like a blow to the gut. The decision to move so late in the fall was a brutal one, surely intended to wipe the people out. Winter would descend upon them in a month—two if they were lucky. The harsh winters that sometimes buffeted the South concerned William most. A stark vision of the elders and small children exposed for months on a thousand-mile walk haunted his dreams and defied every concept of human reason.

Several months had passed since Cheshire County officials turned away from the Cherokee. In the wake of the President's order, the local government publicly encouraged white citizens to encroach on Cherokee communities. Not all of their white neighbors came in armed to plunder and steal, but many did. The land that constituted the Cherokee identity for generations was overtaken within days. Many families were already displaced.

The courts were a last desperate hope for redress, but even the highest tribunal was made impotent in the face of greed. The President, a nativist hero in the eyes of many, challenged the Court to enforce their decision that declared Cherokee sovereignty. In the end, his barbarous estimation proved correct. Sovereignty and the law were toothless lions in the face of a corrupt government and the apathetic masses that propped it up.

A local Cherokee and military man called Jackson Sloan held off some of the violence and destruction of property by agreeing to take a contingent of people and depart in haste. His efforts to assuage the fomenting mob of anti-Cherokee sentiment was rewarded with criminal charges brought against him at the highest levels of state government. Thousands began forming small groups to plan for a departure toward the land of the setting sun.

The promise of a new land in the west was met with considerable doubt. Some argued, and rightly so, that there was no guarantee the new territory would not be taken too once they arrived and settled—that the removal would never cease, and the persecution would persist, until the people found themselves on the shores of the great western ocean. But the few who stayed to fight against the army, led by the prophet Tsali, were hunted down and executed by firing squad. No choice remained for those who wished to survive. They would either leave together or stay to be run down and shot, one by one.

William Reese decided his family would follow Jackson Sloan to the new territory. Sloan was familiar with the route, at least, and a man who could be trusted with their lives. The Reese family waded in that day among their contingent of 356 Cherokees to begin the sad exodus from their home lands into the wilds of Kentucky, Tennessee, Illinois, and then Missouri, on their way to find a new home beyond the borderlands of American civilization.

They were allowed two days to load the wagons at the stockade before the journey began from the Cherokee Agency on October 13, 1837. The first day they crossed the Hiawassee River at Calhoun and set up camp just a few miles past the banks. Rachel Reese spent that first night wrapped in a soft calfskin blanket. She placed a heavy skillet over the fire with a few pieces of pork fat inside. She stared into the flames and listened to the sound of the firewood breaking down into fiery embers. She wondered what the new land looked like. Would this place have cold, clean rivers and streams like the ones back home? Was the evening air in this new place laden with the heady fragrance of magnolia blossoms? She wondered if they would live near a stream like little Peach Eater Creek, which cut its path across the field behind her old house.

Her mother walked up to camp with a draw of water from the river. She set the vessel on the ground and went to her daughter's side.

Rachel's apprehensions were knitted across her dark brow as she stared out over the fire. Her mother's hand wrapped around her waist and reminded her of the love and protection that surrounded them.

Amidst her uncertainties, the greatest plague to Rachel's mind was the health of her grandmother, Mahala. She was the one Rachel favored most. Mahala, the one who taught her to sew and bead her own dresses. The quiet, gentle spirit who patiently guided Rachel's hands to weave baskets from the light-colored reeds they gathered together by the creek. Rachel's heart swelled with emotion at the sight of her grandmother just across the fire, shelling walnuts slowly into the lap of her dress. Her hands were weak and bent with age, but they were precious. Rachel wondered how many hours Mahala's hands had spent at work preparing food for the family or mending a torn dress. During the length of her sixteen years on earth, Rachel had no memory of watching her grandmother use those hands for any task other than to care for her family.

Mahala was a quiet woman who left conversation to others. She was an intent listener. She was a treasure whose wisdom surpassed that of all others in the family taken together. Since the day they left New Echota to gather at the stockade, she had not uttered a word. This did not strike Rachel as particularly strange. Perhaps her grandmother concentrated her energy on survival, or maybe she was still in mourning for the land of her ancestors.

Mahala was far too old to walk the trail to the new territory, so she was given one of the few seats in a wagon along with a few other elderly and infirm. A woman named Eneah sat alongside her. The time for Eneah to give birth was not far away. She took in chilled deep breaths of air and closed her eyes when the pains came. Her other small children were old enough to walk alongside their father. Mahala and Eneah were packed in among the supplies, covered by blankets and material collected in the haste of preparation.

Rachel gave her mother's hand a squeeze and walked over to sit next to Mahala. Their eyes met for a moment and a quiet understanding passed between the two. Rachel picked up a walnut and began to grind apart the shell with a pointed stone.

The next morning, the camp was up and moving at daylight. They packed the provisions back in the wagons and moved out in relative silence. The group covered fourteen miles that first day, despite a trail that led over a hilly land covered in dense forest and underbrush. Their mark for the day was the Tennessee River, and they pushed on until just after dark to reach its banks. Jackson Sloan was determined not to fall behind on the schedule he'd laid out in order to get across the Mississippi before the worst of the winter cold arrived. They were set to cross the Tennessee at daylight the next morning, but the people woke to find a strange and persistent heavy fog settled in the river bottoms. A ferry floated haphazardly at the bank as though impatient for passengers, but it was rendered inoperable and they were unable to move again until late that afternoon. The delay meant only seven miles crossed, despite all their efforts.

The trial of the Cumberland Mountains was the first and most dangerous obstacle of the journey to that point. The group, which seemed so large when they left the foothills of central Georgia, now appeared an insignificant speck in the shadow of the great peaks. The people looked down at their unsuspecting children and considered the great trial that lay before them. Then they raised their heads and marched forward. There was no other way; no turning back.

The air became thinner as the group made their way into the Cumberlands. The lungs of Eneah's baby could not tolerate the conditions. No medicine men traveled with their group, because most had left for the new territory with earlier expeditions. Pneumonia settled in the baby's lungs and Eneah, who braved the pain of his birth surrounded by crates of chickens, barrels of corn, and tins of coffee, spoke a loving farewell in his ear when she knew the end was near. She named him White Hawk and she whispered his name to him over and over again in their language until his lungs pulled in a final rattled breath. There was no time to mourn. Eneah buried White Hawk with a string of beaded leather she wore around her neck. She knelt for just a moment beside the little mound of fresh dirt and then willed herself to walk on with the other two small children who still needed her to survive. After four days, the group emerged. They left behind two elders and four young children on the cold mountainside.

Just on the other side of the pass, they came upon a town where Sloan was able to find additional supplies of corn and bacon. There would be no more fresh water except for the waterways along the route. Despite the treachery of the mountain and the difficult terrain, progress was steady.

On the last sunset of October in 1837, three hundred and thirty-eight Cherokees moved into the hinterlands of Golconda, Illinois. One Golconda resident who witnessed them shuffle past described the sight as a moaning army of ghosts, dressed in rags and dragging the chains of their wagons and animals behind. In the time that stretched between the Cumberland Mountains and the jagged border of Illinois, their number was reduced by another eleven. Inclement weather was not to blame for the most recent deaths. The great majority of the dead were taken now by a fast-spreading wasting disease that ravaged the people without mercy. It brought death to the elders and children, and struck some of the strongest among them with severe dehydration.

Rachel, Ani and William Reese were spared the disease, but Mahala's health was devastated. William kept close to the wagon and walked at his mother's side, flanked by his daughter and wife. Mahala lay covered in blankets. Her frail body deteriorated by the hour. She refused water and food, though both Ani and Rachel implored her to drink.

Sloan entered many of the communities they passed to seek out medicine or the help of a town physician. Most of the Cherokee families had money to pay for help, but they were looked upon by most as diseased vermin. Entire towns refused them entry. These same towns would forbid their own citizens from taking food or medical supplies out to the sick Cherokee, for fear of the rampant contagion rumored to be killing them off.

Rachel began to accept now that her grandmother would not arrive with them in the new territory. They had not yet reached the greatest river, and past that there remained many more days of travel. The group stopped to make camp for the night. The next day, they would cross the Ohio River into Illinois. Rachel knew that when they woke in the morning her beloved Mahala would be gone. Although the night air that blew in off the water caused her to shiver, she took her own blanket and placed it over her grandmother. If Mahala must leave that night, Rachel accepted that the power to stop it was not her own. But she would see at least that her grandmother did not leave the world without knowing warmth.

Mahala opened her eyes and looked up. No recognition could be found in her gaze. She looked past Rachel and up at the stars above.

"U-ne-le. U-ne-le." She whispered again and again.

The words could scarcely be heard but Rachel placed her ear close by and understood. It was the first her grandmother had spoken for many days. She was near death now and spoke of the spirit world, a realm that Rachel herself could not see.

"What light, Grandmother?" Rachel asked, looking up in the direction of Mahala's gaze, as if there might be a light over them in the sky. But there was no light. Even the stars seemed to have hidden themselves away. Rachel turned back to Mahala and laid her soft cheek against the weathered face of her grandmother. She was taken aback by the sensation of bones lying sharp beneath the skin. The cholera had caused her to lose an impossible amount of weight in only a week's time. Rachel was struck by the sudden image of Mahala in the grave. She shook her head to chase away the garish vision and fought against the hot tears that filled her eyes.

Rachel felt suddenly so helpless and alone. She refused to accept that Mahala must leave the world in this way, like an animal abandoned in the cold. She raised her head and looked around for William and Ani. They were nowhere in sight. A thought occurred to her—a call to action. She could run to Golconda and find medicine to save her grandmother. She spoke perfect English—so many Cherokee children had learned to speak and write the white language. She would find someone with medicine and bring them back here to help. Some of the white people were friendly to the Cherokee. Some had even tried to help them resist the removal in the beginning, so she knew they were not all bad. Now, she thought, there was no choice but to find one of them to help save Mahala.

She stood and ran away as fast as her legs would carry her, swift and sure. Away she ran, from the warmth and safety of the campfire toward the distant lights of the town. Her black, waist-length hair whipped in the wind and rapid thuds sounded out, frantic, as her moccasins beat the ground beneath. She spoke low in the wind and beseeched it to carry her to someplace where hope lived.

Rachel ran for almost a mile and a half in the night before she came to a small two-room structure that stood just at the outskirts of Golconda. She ran right up the front step without hesitation and beat on the door with a clenched fist. She felt compelled by some force outside herself.

After a few moments, the front door swung open and there stood a young man in his winter long underwear and nothing more, a candle in one hand and a pistol in the other. It was pointed straight at the center of Rachel's face. His eyes were large with fright.

"What do you want?" He asked.

"Please help me," Rachel cried. She was surprised by the sound of desperation in her own voice. The adrenaline that had pushed her so fast and so far began to wane as the reality of her situation crept to the foremost regions of her mind.

"For God's sake, come in out of the cold." He reached out from the door and grabbed Rachel by the elbow. She followed him blindly inside the home, given over to the idea that either a remedy would be found or she would die trying.

"There is no time," she cried, "I have to go back now; my family will discover that I'm gone and they will come after me."

"God's sake, take some breaths, girl." He still had a grip on her elbow as though she might bolt and run away. "You came from the Indian encampment?"

"Yes," came her simple reply. She was at last beginning to regain breath and mind. "I am the daughter of the Reese family. My grandmother and many of our people are sick. Some are dying and won't live through the night. We need medicine. Can you help us?" She spoke in a long train of un-paused words.

Rachel looked up at his face, and in the dim light of the living room she could see kindness in his eyes despite the shock that remained there. She looked down at the strong hand that secured her arm. He saw her glance and let go. They both felt a surge of electricity pass between their bodies even after the physical contact was ended.

"You put yourself in great danger by approaching this town. Some of the men will shoot on sight if any of you come close."

"Can you help us?" She asked again, standing tall and proud, leaning on the strength of her people. She thought of their life back in Georgia, before she was a mud-covered refugee on the crooked road to a land that no one else wanted.

"I can help," he said. The simple sentence was the loveliest to ever pass through Rachel's conscious mind.

"I must return to my family now," she said. "You will find us at the southern point of the camp. Look for me, I will stand outside our wagon and watch for you. Please hurry."

She turned to leave and he grabbed her elbow once again. Her eyes involuntarily moved from his face to the front of his long underwear and then to the floor. His embarrassment was immediate–in the commotion he had forgotten his own state of undress before a perfect stranger, and a beautiful one at that.

"I'm so sorry," he stammered, turning his body sideways as if to obscure himself. "My name is Thomas Major."

Rachel blushed in return, and her eyes returned to his. She evaluated his appearance. He was square jawed, with a growth of stubble over his chin. His eyes were somehow as dark as her own. They held her fixated and dumb for a short moment. She took in a rapid, deep breath. Even in the desperation of the circumstance, she felt a heat begin to rise in her torso that grew to fill her throat and face. She had never felt anything close to that overwhelming warmth in the presence of another person.

"Rachel. My name is Rachel," she said, and with a quick step she vanished and returned back to the night. The distance had not been so far–she was accustomed to many more miles and her straight, lean body was a testament to that fact. But this time something else drove her to run hard in the direction of her people. Her breaths were rapid and short no matter how she willed her body to calm.

Rachel could see the orange campfires burning off in the distance. They appeared little more than the tiny lights of a hundred candle wicks. A hundred fires blazed on the horizon and a hundred more burned in her gut. Rachel felt it pulling at her, slowing her down, it was a sensation stronger than gravity; a hot weight foreign to her body. He called himself Thomas Major.

She imagined again the moment he opened the door in her mind, standing there in his ridiculous night clothes, the single brass candle holder gripped tight as though it might protect him against whatever evil he imagined outside his door. An undeniable energy was created at the moment of their meeting. There it was; she knew she was meant to find him. The purpose, she was certain, was intervention by the creator, Yowa, to save Mahala's life. But the explanation did not fully satisfy the strange new sensation. A deeper complexity reigned, but she refused its consideration. She decided she must push these strange thoughts far from her conscious mind, but did so with little success. To her alarm, the image of Thomas Major re-appeared in her thoughts over and over again. Her determined direction toward the Cherokee fires and away from his home gave her the temporary comfort that she was still in control of her body at least, even if her mind had begun to unravel.

※ ※ ※

Thomas Major stood still for more than a full minute after the door swung shut, his mind in a confused state. He stared at the unfinished wood before him and summoned again the striking, fiery woman's image who disturbed him from his bed.

His mind was plagued by a swarm of questions all tripping over one other in a frantic state of reproduction. Who was she? How did this Indian possess the courage to nearly beat down a white man's door, demanding anything at all besides a bullet in the head? He had watched the people stagger past on the way to their camp earlier that day. The mere sight of them made him sick with pity. By his estimation, only an animal might fail to be moved by their plight.

This had been the extent of his consideration for the Cherokee until now. They had seemed an unfortunate lot sent to die in the frozen wilderness, where no civilized people would have to watch. But now there was this one. This girl. A determined will lived in her eyes, and an unfamiliar strength accompanied her presence. She was not to be pitied. She was strong and unafraid of the people that should have been feared the most. A brown girl with sad and serious eyes who dared to demand his help.

With that thought, he became aware of the need to move. He turned and rushed to the storage box that sat on his bedroom floor. Inside he kept stacks of medicine, stored since his service in the U.S. Army. Medicine had been issued to each man to stave off the contagious diseases that spread through their ranks, though Thomas had never required its administration. He was uncommonly healthy, and as far back as his memory served he had never been stricken with so much as a common cold. He kept the medicine in hopes that it might be put to good use some day; perhaps in aid of an ill neighbor or sick child in town.

But the time was now, and the Cherokees had sent this girl, a woman really—for no girl could have taken off to do what she had done—who appeared like a vision to tell him what he had to do. And damn it if he didn't find himself rushing around to do exactly what she said. He didn't know what might come of the circumstances, but he believed and oft repeated the saying that God works in mysterious ways. Now he only knew that he had to find his way back into Rachel's presence again, at least one more time, if only to convince himself that the curious feeling she aroused in him had not been the trickery of a sleep-addled mind at the sight of a surreal Cherokee princess alight on his step in the night.

Thomas stuffed the lot of the medicine into a leather satchel. His work shirt and denims were draped on the foot of the bed and he hurried to pull them on. He walked in a rush to the stove and stepped into his boots. They were warm and he took a moment to enjoy the heat before it began to dissipate with each step he took away from the fire and toward the darkness outside. He thought of taking his horse from the barn out back and then thought better of it. She could very well step in a hole and break a leg on the way. He would cover the distance on foot. If a young girl could make her way across this land in the dark, well then, so could he.

Major stepped out from his warm front room and into the chilly night air. The leather satchel of medicine was slung low across his hip. He began to walk—not at a quick pace but a steady one—in the direction of the campgrounds. He remembered to carry an oil lamp along the way. He couldn't be of help to anyone if he fell out there in the dark. Some kind of light was needed to reveal the path to this girl and her people.

Rachel saw a flurry of activity outlined in the darkness ahead. Indistinct figures moved in and out of the fire's illumination. She could not see their faces. The movement occurred at a frantic pace, and Rachel feared she was too late to save Mahala. She began to run again, focused now only on reaching her family. Lit torches bobbed up and down in the air like tiny flaming moons.

One of the young boys spotted her and began to shout as she neared camp. "Rachel returns from the darkness!"

She heard the voice of her mother calling out praise to Yowa for Rachel's return. William Reese reached her first and grabbed her by the shoulders.

"Where have you gone?" He demanded in a combination of fear and relief.

"I am sorry, Father, I did not want to frighten you. I left to find help. I ran almost all the way to the town in search of medicine for Mahala."

The anger left William's face, replaced by gratitude. He let go of her shoulders and took a step back so they could walk into the camp where the others waited.

Rachel wasted no time on any of them. She rushed to the wagon and peered over the side. Though the people gathered around had caused her to fear she was too late, she saw that Mahala was still with them. She took in the relief that came with the sight of her grandmother's sweet face, looking up at the sky from the edge of her quilts.

Rachel saw that many of the people who had gathered around now returned to their own campfires. She realized only then that her father had been in the process of organizing a search. Men were dousing out makeshift torches. A few snuffed out oil lamps, relieved that one of their own was not lost and left alone out in this dark foreign land.

Rachel turned to William and Ani and began to tell about her run in the night and how she had found, as if guided by the Spirit, the home of a white medicine man, and that he agreed to bring his medicine back for Mahala.

"Why have you done this without first speaking of it to us?" Ani asked. "Mahala would never ask you to disregard your own life on such a foolish journey and if you had not returned from the darkness you would have brought death upon her just the same."

Ani's voice rose with anger as she spoke, because she saw that Rachel was no longer listening. Instead, the girl was staring off into the night. Rachel's respect for her family had never faltered before, and Ani realized that her daughter was changed. She left the camp as their young girl and somehow returned transformed. Even the shape of her face had shifted from its youthful roundness into the willful, determined lines of a woman.

Ani looked out in the direction of Rachel's stare and saw movement off in the dark. At first she picked up a brief flash, so insignificant that it might have been a trick of the imagination. For a moment, Ani thought of the faint lights of fireflies, and their scores of tiny beacons that winked off and on over fields of fresh clover in the hot summertime. But now they were gone, their greenish glow snuffed out by the onset of the winter months. She realized that something or someone was out in the distant night, moving steadily toward camp.

As the light neared, it became more consistent, burning stronger until Ani saw that a man walked toward them carrying a lamp. Rachel said nothing at first, only stared with wide eyes that glittered like dark jewels. After a few moments, she managed a single sentence in explanation:

"This is the light of Thomas Major."

※ ※ ※

Major introduced himself right away to William Reese, who was as surprised as the rest at the sight of the white man. They had been warned of the dark sentiment of the townspeople, and this lantern approached from their direction. William considered the notion that the carrier of this light might bring trouble.

Major did not hesitate and spoke to William with humility and respect. "Mr. Reese, I am certain that my presence here is of no comfort to you. But you have my word that I am only here to help." He paused in his rapid speech at Rachel's appearance. He forced himself to retrain his gaze on William.

"Your daughter Rachel came to tell me that your people are in trouble. My name is Thomas Major. I brought all the medicine I have."

William returned the greeting with an equal measure of formality: "We are grateful that you would leave your home to walk in the dark to help us. Please forgive my daughter. She was stricken with grief by the sight of her grandmother's illness."

Major pulled the brown leather satchel from across his shoulders and lifted the overlapping cover. He motioned for William to look inside. "I have enough here to help many people," he explained, "but I'm afraid it won't be enough for everyone."

He held the lamp so it shone down into the bag and illuminated the contents. William could not mask the emotion he felt at the sight of it. This man was right: the medicine was not enough to help all who were dying, but he was certain that some would be saved by this stranger's kindness.

"Thank you for this gift," William told him.

Ani took the medicine and mixed it in a pot of boiling water that hung over the fire. The vessel had been used earlier that night to warm their dinner, but now instead of the smell of stewing potatoes and pork, the steam that rose carried a bitter, metallic odor.

William Reese invited Major to remain with them there until the next morning, while the medicines were distributed among the sick and dying. Rachel made a comfortable place for Major next to the fire. She was calm and collected by all outward appearances, but inside she felt she had swallowed a handful of moths. She knelt beside him and lowered her eyes to the ground. "My father says I should apologize for disturbing you. And I *am* sorry for speaking to you as I did. Now that you are here, you can see the reason for my lack of manners. I hope you will forgive me and accept my gratitude."

Major sat still and listened, though as he did he took inventory of the untamed beauty that sat before him. The electrical energy that sparked between them at their first meeting was renewed and intensified. Neither tried to make excuses or push it away this time. An innate magnetism was present that would not be denied.

"You don't owe me a single thing," he said.

Rachel knew that other people were moving in and out of the surrounding periphery, but all was a blur. She only saw Major.

Time rushed past in earnest, and the first rays of light gathered and spilled unexpectedly over the eastern rim of the earth. They tumbled over into Rachel's new world like a waterfall of prisms, illuminating all that surrounded her in a dazzling light. Neither Major not Rachel slept or realized the hours absorbed by the vortex of their hastened exchange of stories in the night. They became aware now that time was a deathly enemy that would soon usher in their premature dissolution. William and Ani watched at a distance and waited, with the understanding that at the sun's ascension they would move forward with their daughter and this man would return back to his home. Ani supposed that Rachel's thirst to know this white man would be satisfied in those hours few, and afterward they would move on without consequence.

But in truth, the vast amount of knowledge exchanged between the two in that short span of time was more than enough to fill a book. Rachel came to know that Major's parents were both dead— his father had gone first, then his mother when he was only a boy of thirteen. He had worked a number of jobs to feed himself and keep his family home, and had joined the United States Army once he was able. From there, he had saved enough to return home and make a decent existence for himself off of the land.

The interruption of the sunrise was beautiful and savage, given the terrible realization that the circumstances that brought them together would now serve as the dreaded scene of their parting. The sounds of people beginning to stir surrounded them. Soon it would be time for the Cherokee to move on.

"Stay here with me," he demanded. "You love me already; I know it."

She shook her head in automatic refusal, and it was like a screw twisted in his heart.

"I can never leave my family," said Rachel. "And you understand they would never leave here without me either. I must go with them..." Her voice trailed off and she waited, hoping Major would pick up the rest of her sentence.

After a second's hesitation, he did, though it was a rather unusual pause indeed. In that pause, that single tick of eternity's stubborn clock—just a grain of sand in an ocean of time—an eternity of these had been so casually discarded. But within this particular pause, a lifetime of Major's own past played a silent movie in its entirety. In just a single second he knew how damned foolish his past was, and in some way felt he was watching the scene before him outside his own body, in a cool and detached manner. This sole exchange between a woman and a man. During this one second, he saw all the times he had spent leaving or being left. Sometimes these exits were for a purpose—the time spent at war, for example—but others by happenstance. *Oh, Mother, my dear, sweet mother,* he thought.

Major realized then that too much—a great percentage of his young life in fact—had already been spent on losing love. He made the decision—an unshakable one—that now, the present, was the opportunity sent his way by the Almighty to turn it all around. Here was the chance to begin to change those percentages of sorrow into a number much more in favor of joy and a life lived well, without regret. He would not ignore this one, nor allow it to escape him. In that single second, in both the instant and the eternity of it, Thomas Major changed his own fate and swung his path to cross directly with many others still untold.

The speed with which Major replied shocked Rachel, for in her mind less than a full second had passed before he spoke. All was a matter of perception. But the words flowed involuntarily from some deep part of his soul. A fear had been concealed there in those depths. It was a fear born of man's ageless search for that part of him that had always been missing. And only a matter of hours ago that part had walked in out of the darkness and materialized at his door. The possibility that she might disappear again was a prospect much too desperate for the man to consider.

"I will come after you, then. Give me one week to arrange my affairs here. Yes, I will come after you. I know the only route to the Mississippi River from Port Royal. Your people will pass through

Golconda and travel on to the river." He spoke his plans aloud, as much to himself as to her. "I'll meet you on the banks of the Mississippi prior to your crossing."

Rachel was stunned at the sudden proposition. "I don't understand how you will ever find us again," she said.

"Rachel, so many of you are travelling together. Trust me. I will find you. Wait for me. I will bring my horses and wagon and all that I own that will fit inside. When I find you, I will discuss our marriage with your mother and father. We can make a life and a family together in your new land. Believe in my promise."

She could not understand why, but in a single night she had come to trust Thomas Major more than any other. Evidence of his passion and sincerity lay in his eyes. His voice carried the truth of his intent within. And so Rachel found herself nodding her head to let him know she would wait for his return. A further exchange of words became unnecessary, so he imparted a solitary kiss upon her upturned cheek and walked away.

The din of the Cherokee's great number was a bitter farewell song for Major. The return walk stretched out before him much farther than it had the night before. For the first time since his mother died, he felt truly and abjectly alone. Not lonely, for that was a passing state of mind that struck every man from time to time. Lonely was a temporary condition that could be cured with the passage of time. Now Major realized that he was wholly alone, and the knowledge that he was moving away from Rachel Reese rained over him with the violence of a late summer storm. He had to settle matters at home first. Only a vagrant with no past and no hope of a future would conduct himself otherwise, and he was a prudent, reasonable man. Still, emotion welled up in his chest and fear that he might never see her again gnawed at his mind. The only available solace lived in the mental image of his little house outside Port Royal all boarded up, with the moving picture of himself set out across the land to reunite with his life's greatest love.

Chapter 4

Shell

> *There's a killer on the road.*
> *His brain is squirming like a toad.*
> The Doors, "Riders on the Storm"

The blacktop maintained a tight grip on the curves of the countryside; its white lines rose and fell with the hills in the distance. Len and Shell rode in perfect silence for the first twenty miles or so. Shell stuck her elbow in the crook where the window met the door and rested her chin on a clenched fist. She gazed out, watching nothing in particular but the brown-green blur of grass and trees and fences racing off in the opposite direction.

Len was a horrid backseat driver and complained without ceasing when Shell drove, so she preferred him behind the wheel. He sat at a near ninety-degree angle, hands locked on at ten and two, eyes directed at the highway dead ahead. Never one for lengthy silences, he reached with one hand toward the console for Shell's purse.

"Hey, where'd you put the playlist I made for the trip?"

"Should be there," she replied. She reached over and took the purse from him and rifled through its contents. "Here it is," she said, handing over the black iPod. She pushed the adapter into the cigarette lighter on the dash and asked, "What do you want to hear first?"

"They go in order. Just start it from the first and let it play through."

"In order? In order of what?" she asked. Her dark red thumbnail spun round and round on the screen until she scrolled down to the title, *ROADTRIP*. She pushed the center button and waited.

As soon as the first notes passed into her ears, Shell recognized the spacey piano opening of her favorite album, *Will O' the Wisp*.

"Perfect!" Shell said, delighted, "I haven't heard this one in a long time. The soundtrack for our trip."

Len took his eyes off of the road to watch her reaction. He was happy to see she was pleased. She turned to him and flashed her broad smile, her eyes crinkling at the corners. Her smile was a little crooked, one side tilted up a fraction more than the other. Her teeth were off-center too, but despite all the imperfections, or perhaps because of them, she was an attractive woman.

Shell crossed her legs. Her foot bounced in the air in time with the music and she threw her head back and howled, "*Hold on to that feeling. Can you FEEL IT?*" Shell couldn't hold a note, and her tone was atrocious, but Len thought it was nice at last to see a shift in her pensive mood.

He refocused his attention on the road. The longest part of their journey still lay ahead. A mile or so in the distance, a succession of brake lights flashed red, one after another.

"Must be a wreck up there."

"Where?" Shell asked, and jumped to attention. She craned her neck forward to get a better look.

"Well, I'm not certain it's a wreck, but look at that traffic."

As they topped a small rise in the interstate, she could see the traffic yawning out for what looked like miles, far past the greatest reach of her vision.

"Oh, no." Shell picked up her phone and began dialing.

"Who are you calling?"

"I want to call my parents and let them know we won't be in 'til late."

"It might not be that bad, Shell; why don't you just wait and see how long it takes to get through?"

"Look at that, Len," she said, gesturing ahead at the endless line of cars. "There isn't an exit for miles, and no one's moving an inch."

"Fine, call. What's the difference."

"Shhhhhh!" She clamped her left hand over her ear. The phone trilled in her ear three times.

"Hey Sis!" It was her father's gravelly voice.

"Hi, Dad, whatcha doin'?"

"Oh, we're just sittin' here waiting on you. We're awful lonesome."

"Me too. I can't wait to see you guys. Well, I say that, but it looks like we'll have to wait a little longer than expected. You wouldn't believe the traffic we just ran into."

"Traffic?" Shell heard the tone of his voice tick up an octave in concern. "What's the deal?"

"We don't know. Len thinks it's a wreck, could be construction though. We can't see the end of it yet, but either way it's going to set us back. If we don't make it by bedtime, don't wait up."

"Okay, but drive careful and buckle up. Send a text when you get out of traffic, so we'll have some idea of when to expect you."

"No problem, I'm hoping we…" Shell's sentence trailed off as they inched by a state trooper standing outside his cruiser, parked on the grassy shoulder of the road. The blue and white lights revolved, alternating one after another atop the cab. As the officer spoke into the radio at his shoulder, his eyes darted along the line of traffic and met Shell's gaze. His eyebrows were raised and one arm moved up and down in nervous chopping motions as he spoke. Shell guessed from his demeanor that Len was right; there must have been a terrible accident ahead.

"You still there, Shell?" Dean Foster's voice shot like an arrow through her fogged imagination.

"Oh yeah, sorry. We just drove by a cop and I was distracted for a sec."

"Jeez, it's the coppers." This was his unfailing joke any time he caught sight of, or heard mention of, the police.

"Yeah, it's the coppers, and I'd better get off here, Dad. I'll call you as soon as we're clear of it. Love you. Bye." She closed the phone and dropped it back into the cup holder.

Shell's father was a hardworking man blessed with a highly developed intellect. He had always held a blatant contempt for the local police force. As a young man, besting the police was some of the greatest entertainment he could drum up out in the country. He was fond of picking up a few cold beers at the corner store for the drive home from work each day, and, on occasion, he might pull out a joint from the seat cover of his old Chevy pickup. The police pulled him over and cited him a few times. They even suspended his license once. People in the community with nothing better to do whispered that Dean Foster was hell-bent. But out of some sense of indignant righteousness, Dean held fast to his old habits. He enjoyed a good game of cat and mouse.

Shell thought back to one of her earliest memories with her father. She had been riding with him on the highway that ran between town and home. They were in the same old Chevy pickup. She had just celebrated her eleventh birthday the previous week. They were barreling down the winding two lane blacktop through the countryside. The truck didn't have air-conditioning, so the windows were rolled down and Shell sat staring out at the blur of passing trees and the occasional farmhouse. Distracted, she failed to notice a patrol car cruise by in the opposite direction.

"Shit," Dean Foster said. His foot smashed down like an anchor on the gas pedal.

"What is it, Dad?"

"Put your seat belt on," he replied, eyes fixed on the rearview mirror.

Shell stared straight ahead at the rapidly disappearing yellow lines on the roadway. She knew by the strange pitch of her father's voice that something was wrong. When the truck picked up speed and Dean shifted into the highest gear, Shell reached her hands out and gripped the dashboard.

Her curiosity was satisfied when she heard the whir of a police siren howling behind them. Revolving blue lights reflected onto her face from the side mirror as the officer jerked his car into a driveway to turn around.

Her father never said another word. As the truck accelerated to its maximum speed, Shell's stringy brown hair became a torrent, whipping in the wind. She was blinded for a moment. Reaching across her right shoulder, she quickly grabbed the latch on the shoulder harness and slung the belt across her body, snapping it into the buckle in one smooth motion. A lucky shot, no doubt. Finally, both hands were free, and she reached in the air to grab handfuls of flying hair and hold it all in a haphazard bun behind her head.

Without warning her father, with a stoned and steely resolve, Shell hit the knob on the dash and shut off the headlights. Without once touching the brakes, her father cut a hair pin ninety-degree turn to the left, down a scarcely traveled gravel road. Suddenly the truck was barreling down the dark lane in the heavy blackness of the summer night.

Shell turned to look behind them. Just as she turned, she saw the colorful twirling lights of the police car streak past. The cop never saw them turn off the highway. He had no clue where they had gone.

Dean touched the brakes and the truck began to slow until at last he threw the gear shift into park. Only the toads and locusts from a nearby creek bank croaked in protest. Shell sat there on the edge of the worn Chevy bench seat, eyes dilated and round as saucers, her fingertips still pressed into the dashboard. A crescent moon sat low in the southeastern sky and shed the faintest bath of light over the darkened countryside. She was at once terrified and elated.

Dean Foster took in a deep breath and looked over at Shell with a giant smile on his face. "You okay?"

She nodded back at him in the dark, reassured by the ease of his demeanor. That night had happened well over twenty years ago, but the imprint of it remained in her memory as vivid as if it was just yesterday.

An eighteen-wheeler eased in front of Len from an on-ramp. The truck driver steadied his load in front of them. A distorted image of their car was mirrored back at them from the shiny aluminum doors on the back of the trailer. Their faces were not recognizable in the reflection, just two dark forms staring back at themselves in a fun house mirror.

Oh, you said you was never intendin' to break up the feeling this way, but there ain't any use in pretending, it could happen to us any day. The steady bass line rumbled over the speakers as the traffic began to move forward at a steady pace. Up ahead, Shell could just see the outline of a single silver sedan overturned on the shoulder. The driver's side of the car was smashed in.

An ambulance sat nearby, its lights and sirens turned off.

"Now there's something you never want to see at a car wreck," said Len.

"What is it?"

"There's a reason the ambulance is just sitting there," said Len matter-of-factly. "It means whoever was in that wreck is dead on the scene."

Shell looked out her window as they crept by. Between the car and the ambulance, a small pale gray blanket lay on the ground.

That can't possibly be big enough to cover an entire person, she thought. She turned sideways in her seat to get a better look. As the car inched closer, it became obvious that there was indeed a body beneath the blanket. She was struck by an immediate sense of sorrow for the unknown person lying there.

A strong breeze picked up and the trees in the median bowed toward the ground. One of the officers working the accident hastily snatched at his paperwork before it could blow away.

Shell kept staring at the covered body. Suddenly, the strong winds whipped back the blanket to expose the victim. His brutalized body was wrenched at a strange angle. The head faced in Shell's direction, although the shoulders were turned opposite. A jagged gash zippered its way back from the victim's temple, spanning his entire forehead. A compound fracture jutted its way out of the skin at his collarbone. His lips were pulled back, exposing a tight, toothy grimace.

Was this a manifestation of fear? She wondered. *A last conscious expression frozen on his face at the realization he had lost all measure of control?*

But it was the dead man's eye that struck her as the most fearsome sight. One was not visible because of swelling and blood. The other, however, remained open and appeared to be focused on some sight unseen in the distance. Shell found she could not break her gaze. She was suddenly struck by a desperate need to know the man's name. Surely his family loved him. She wondered what had occupied his thoughts just before the car went out of control. *A long lost love? An unpaid bill?*

Just as this last thought passed through her mind, the eye, for a single second, became furiously animated, darting this way and that, furious in its lone search for a final resting place. The horror of it was perhaps not so much the movement of his eye as it was the stillness of his rest. After the desperate, wretched pursuit, the eye finally settled on Shell. The very moment it locked upon her own eyes, the pupil dilated and the man's head lolled downward with a sickening lack of restraint, not more than a couple of centimeters, and his taut expression relaxed. The movement was barely discernible.

"My God, Len, did you see that?"

"Yeah, it was awful," he said distracted. He was focused on the road again.

"No, I mean that man. The dead man. He *moved*." After the scene back at the house, Shell restrained herself from explaining that a dead man had just made eye contact, though she felt a smothering sense of panic and felt a cold sweat begin to bead up across her face.

"Shell, did you see that guy's head? It was caved in like an eggshell. You might have seen movement, but it wasn't because he was still alive. His nerves were still firing, no doubt. That happens sometimes for minutes after a person dies."

"I want to go back and tell the paramedics so they can be sure."

"One thing's sure, babe." Len placed his hand on her knee. "That guy's a goner. I'm sure the paramedics have it under control. Think of it this way: he's one of the lucky ones. It probably happened so quick, he didn't feel a thing. Hey, you wanna know the last thing that went through his mind before he hit that windshield?"

"My God, what is wrong with you? How could you say something like that?"

"Just trying to lighten the mood, Shell, damnit. I don't understand why anytime we encounter some insignificant event, you feel the need to add in your own supernatural BS and go dramatic. You're crazy. I mean, I really think you have a mental illness! It's a goddam dead guy on the road. What the hell do you want me to do?" A grim look overtook his entire countenance.

The traffic began to clear up ahead. As soon as they were out of sight of the Highway Patrol, Len dropped a heavy foot on the accelerator.

He felt like he was running out of answers. Nothing he ever did brought a thing from Shell except more bitching and moaning. Her angst had come on months before, and only seemed to worsen with time. He was certain she had flipped her lid a little, and he found her behavior toward him inexcusable. He felt it impossible to take a single step without somehow pissing her off. At best she was disinterested, and during the worst of times he sensed resentment at his very presence. The one thing he knew for sure was that he had not changed. The difference could only be attributed to Shell. Of course, he thought, her attitude now was somewhat reminiscent of the first time he saw her. Back then she hadn't even bothered to notice he was alive.

They had both been on campus. Both neared graduation and were well past the self-conscious patter that plagued most undergraduate students. Len had his ten year plan on track. The university atmosphere had been new and stimulating in the first year, but now in his last it was all spent and dull. When he watched new freshmen crossing the green oval of the commons, crowding the heels of their guide and scribbling notes at every word, Len was annoyed. A giant gap of experience and knowledge separated him from these people, and he felt a strong desire to break ties with any institution to which they belonged.

This last semester was kind of a coast. Other than his senior thesis in government administration he was home free. After that was behind him it would be time to pack up his things and return to Boston. Thank God, Boston. The idea of leaving this hick state in the dust was like a dream he feared might never come to fruition. The full scholarship was really not worth the extreme culture shock of migrating from an eastern city to live here among these slow, aggressively friendly people. He longed to return to a place where he was not obliged to return the wave or nod of a complete stranger, or hear the heavy dripping Oklahoma accents. How refreshing it would be to escape all the gravy and cheeses and consequently burgeoning asses. He couldn't wait to see the place in his rearview.

His desire to return to Boston was not driven by a need to get back to his family. God, no, although they would come in handy if he had difficulty with the job hunt at first. He was ready to return to the network of the old neighborhood around him. Back home, at least, he still had a few good buds he could count on. Len was happy that the university had provided him with a full ride, because now he would not be forced to begin adult life upside down fifty grand. He'd just never been able to master the social mannerisms of this place. Even in the diversity of the college, he never discovered a niche that felt comfortable. Most regarded his thick Boston accent as a novelty, and laughed when he spoke. As far as any close friends were concerned, he was out.

He had been in a hurry to get to his oceanography class that morning, a waste-of-time elective thrown in at the last minute because it fit the gap in his schedule. But then he noticed a woman sitting outside the union, by herself, with a book and a cigarette. Even now he could not say for sure what it was about her that made him stop, start again, then stop and stand in place with an unabashed stare.

Maybe the draw was that she seemed so distant and insulated, alone in that hustling crowd, just like himself. But he felt no sense that he should feel sorry for her at all or try and offer his company. She had set her bag on the opposite chair at the table. He was not lost on the message. It was a sign to passersby that she was just fine, thank you, and no, she was not interested in company or conversation.

She was tall, but Leonard couldn't see just how. He only knew that her crossed legs stretched out beneath the table and their length matched that of the table top above. Three-and-a-half feet or four, maybe. She was taller than most women, no doubt. Her hair was very dark, nearly black, though the weak sunshine betrayed a barely discernible reddish tint. The length of it was swept back in a careless fashion, pinned in a strange quasi-bun at the crown of her head with untidy pieces poking out here and there. A black pen stuck out of the top of all this, jabbed up there in a hurry after class, no doubt. Apparently this girl wasn't all too concerned with her appearance; a fact that made her altogether more distinct from the great migration of cookie-cutter tarts who stampeded and tripped across the commons in groups of three or more like frightened wildebeest, clutching their phones like a crucifix and giggling nervously amongst themselves.

Leonard felt himself frozen, as though his feet were stuck in heavy wet cement for what must have been an entire minute, standing there behind her less than twenty yards away. She never looked up and he was glad for that, though she surely must have felt the sense of someone's eyes upon her. A handful of harried students rushed past, one or two of them taking brief notice of his lonely dark-haired smoker. He felt an insane spark of jealousy jolt through him as though no one else was allowed to look at this girl but him. *What the hell is wrong with me?* he wondered.

She never did look behind to see the figure standing there. Leonard was now quite late but he could not concern himself with class at the moment. He felt a compulsion to approach her. Perhaps she would invite him to sit down. He rather absently placed a hand upon his empty breast pocket and wished he had not forgotten his shades that day. The girl (well, woman, really) was wearing hers after all. Another weapon in her anti-social arsenal.

Maybe she would not mind so much if he just made a quick introduction of himself and then moved on. Damn, it was so bright outside, he thought. It was the first unofficial day of spring, when the sun at last began to warm the air, rather than just shine there cold and passive in the sky. The wind still carried a chill, and Leonard noticed when it blew that the girl would wrap her free hand, the one that didn't hold a book and a smoke, tight against her waist, embracing herself.

"Hey, I'd like to do that for you," he imagined himself saying. Len shook the cheesy line from his head. He realized that he had to make a move, and soon. He felt that he was a bit of an eyesore standing in the same spot with a faceless crowd streaming before and behind him.

He was no novice at approaching women. Most of the time it was all a numbers game, anyway. Approach enough of them and eventually you find a taker. This time, though, he did not feel motivated by the need for a short-term ego boost for the night. There was a different feeling about this one, as if he felt the heavy hand of fate upon him, pushing him in her direction. *Why this one?* He thought. He usually preferred blondes.

At long last, and at great risk of rejection, he began to walk toward her. She had her back to him all the while, and he was filled with icy anticipation at the thought of what the full view of her face might look like. Just as he approached, the girl must have reached a stopping point in the book because she took in a heavy sigh, as though she wished the story had not been interrupted, and stuck a used post-it note on the page to mark her place.

Leonard could not remember a person who moved at such a decisive pace—or maybe it was just that his own movement was so slow. Either way, the dark haired girl dashed her book and cigarettes in her bag, threw its strap over her shoulder, and was off in the crowd of students before he could reach her. He watched as she walked away. Her long legs covered a lot of ground, but she was still easy to spot from a hundred yards away. She stood a head above every other woman.

Len was sorely disappointed that he had missed the chance to introduce himself, but felt sure he would see her again. And when he did, he promised himself, there would be no more hesitation. He had to know her for reasons he did not yet comprehend.

That night, she was in his brain like a stubborn song stuck on repeat over and over again. He hardly slept, because the star of his imaginary movie was always walking away, playing across the big screen of his mind, the only feature in town. He decided to find her the next day. He would skip all of his classes and wait for her to walk by the student union again. She probably passed through every day on her lunch hour. A creature of habit, he was sure.

The next morning he got up with a rushed sense about him, as if he had to get to this mystery woman to meet his fate. He dismissed any cautionary thoughts that she might reject him or, even worse, ignore him and walk away again. He would *make* her take notice. Leonard went to the student union armed with several issues of *The Economist* that he'd always intended to read but never had, and a book on the Soviet Union he had already finished. He had not retained any information from it other than the words *glasnost* and *perestroika*, and he could never remember which one meant "openness" and which meant "restructuring" anyway. He just hoped that if she did notice him—if this woman took an interest—she would be impressed by his reading selections.

By the noon hour, Len felt a little anxious, ready for her to appear. He had not read a word of his magazines for fear he might miss her. He caught sight of a tallish brunette once, and his heart flopped like a fish in his chest, but then she walked on and he saw from her shoulder-length hair and choppy gait that she was not the One.

Lunchtime came and went. Len began to get annoyed and desperate. But what if he gave up and left, and she happened through? That, he thought, would be apropos and in line with the typical Leonard Harris hard-luck story. He decided to remain there for the rest of the day. The reward would be well worth the wait. But she never came. At five o'clock, long after most students were vacated from both the union and the campus, he resigned. If only, he thought, he had acted on that first impulse when she was within reach. He could have caught her in time if he had not been so hesitant and slow. He slumped back to his little two-room flat overlooking college square, and sat in his shorts watching television to numb the sting of failure.

The next morning, he woke and went through the usual rituals of his daily routine. The only medicine for his ailment, he was sure, would be a return to normalcy. He felt so stupid.

He decided not to appear in the union that day, as some sort of lesson for conducting himself in such a foolish manner the day before. But when he sat near the final minutes of admin class, his stomach registered a protest that rang out loud enough for several students in close proximity to hear. He clapped his hand over his stomach and blushed. Then he rubbed his hand over his stomach in great exaggerated circles to show his classmates these were growls of hunger and not gas. When the professor released them from class, Len headed straight for the union with a design on a to-go carton of Chinese food.

He walked in through the south doors, toward the little gathering of fast food restaurants at the north end of the building. When he walked past the giant glass pane windows that looked out on the grass and tables outside, he had to blink three times to make sure they were not mistaken. There she was. Right there at the same table again, with her bag on the chair and her nose in a book.

Of course, you dumb patsy, he told himself. *She's on a Monday-Wednesday-Friday schedule. She had no reason to be at the union yesterday.*

He moved without hesitation, determined not to squander another chance. She would not get away from him this time.

"Hey, those things'll kill ya," he offered, and plopped down at the table. She hardly looked up, annoyed that anyone missed the glaring hints that she sat alone by choice.

"No kidding?" she replied without even a hint of humor. "You know, guy, you're the first person to ever tell me that? Thanks." She stood up at once and ground out her Marlboro Light in the heaping ashtray.

He called after her, desperate, "Hey, what's your name?"

She paused just one step and called back, "My name is Shell. What's yours?"

He was elated by the sound of her voice and the fact that she hadn't yet walked away.

"It's Leonard Harris. Len to you, Beautiful," came the reply. She turned and walked away through the revolving door and out of earshot.

What a jackass, she thought to herself, but she couldn't help smiling at his parting remark. Too much time had passed since she had heard a compliment from the opposite sex, and his admiration provided a fleeting balm for her damaged ego, which was still sore from her divorce.

When she entered her second year of college, Shell had met an older man at a party and was caught up in a whirlwind romance. Despite her declaration to never do so, she was married by the end of the year. He supported her while she pursued her education, and the marriage ran along steadily. But when she neared graduation the relationship suffered, and the tedious emotional connection that held them together eroded with such rapidity that it was over before either of them were aware of how it all happened.

After three months of half-hearted attempts to save the marriage, they both resigned to the loss. The relationship came to a close with more of a whimper than a bang. He moved on seamlessly with another woman, and Shell threw herself into the completion of her nursing degree despite repeated pleas from her family to come back home.

It was during this time of emotional upheaval that Shell took notice of Leonard Harris. He seemed to appear out of the periphery, unashamedly cracking lame jokes and blatantly flirting to hold her attention. He was tall and lean, with brown eyes that held a mischievous sparkle, determined to inject himself into her life at any cost. Every day when she went to her spot outside the union, there he was, waiting.

Over the next several weeks, Shell began to look forward to Len's company. He had what seemed to be an unending supply of interesting stories and inappropriate jokes. His litany of tales never waned, and he possessed a seemingly infinite desire to talk. On occasion, she caught herself drifting off during some of his lengthier speeches, but for the most part Len Harris became a welcome distraction.

One day in the middle of a fifteen-minute yarn, Len came to a dead stop in mid-sentence. He reached out and grabbed Shell's wrist from across the table. It startled her, and she looked at him in confusion. This was the first time he'd dared to make physical contact.

"Listen to me," he said, with the springtime sun blazing in his face. His gaze held an intense determination she had never seen in him before.

"Look," he said, "I know you've been through it lately. Your eyes give you away. For once, Shell, why don't you let someone take care of you? Come over to my place tonight. I'll cook dinner and put on a movie. We'll just relax. What's your favorite wine? I'll get a bottle, and you can take it easy for once. There's no pressure, no expectations. Just a night to take your mind off of things. Plus, it couldn't hurt to get to know me a little better away from this place. Come on; please just give it a chance."

Shell looked back at him, calculating. In the wake of her divorce, she was ambivalent about the idea of investing in a new relationship. She understood her initial hesitancy to mean that it was still much too early to date again. Taking a chance with someone new seemed a daunting proposition guaranteed to end badly.

A brisk gust of wind stirred the pile of leaves beneath their bench in a slow circle. The breeze blew cold against her outstretched legs.

"Shell?" Leonard's deep voice shattered her thought process like a hammer to glass.

"What? Yes! Yes, I mean, sure, why not. Dinner sounds great," Shell stammered, unsettled.

Len's grip tightened around her wrist. His eyes gleamed eager. "You won't be sorry."

He took out a sheet of paper and wrote down his address. Shell stuck it in the front zipper of her backpack and slung it over her arms. She stood and began to make her way across the grassy section to the parking lot.

"See you tonight, Beautiful," he called after her. Shell's right hand absently encircled her left wrist, gently touching its fleshy underside at the place where Len had demanded her attention. She wondered just exactly who she had gotten herself involved with.

That night he spoke nearly the entire time. Hardly a second intervened in conversation. He told her stories about growing up in the city; stories that rang foreign in her ears since she had only ever lived in the vast countryside until her move to the college town. While he cooked their meal and uncorked a bottle of wine, his mouth never stopped going as he discussed his parents and siblings, then moved on to his brief stint in the military before he came to Oklahoma on scholarship. Some women might have been put off by his talkative nature and apparent preoccupation with the sound of his own voice, but not Shell. She was relieved to sit there quietly, sipping on a nice glass of French red wine while he talked. A sense of relief washed over her just to have someone else volunteer for all of the responsibility. If Leonard had not insisted upon the date she would have been satisfied to remain on her own, but at this point in her life she just did not have the energy or will to resist his advances.

Len fed upon her attention like a man starved. Shell made him feel just like a slow, hot fire was building inside, and every time he paused to see her sitting there, watching him cook and engaged in his stories, it was like she tossed another piece of kindling on the flames. She was just what he needed, and by some miracle he saw in her returned gaze that she must be interested in him too.

Shell was all too aware that the timing of their new relationship was most regrettable, and that the rebound syndrome would likely have both of them bitter when it was over. But for the moment she was distracted and entertained by the company of a man, and he kept her plied with an arsenal of compliments. Len was the perfect prescription for her divorce-addled ego.

The typical rites of courtship were skirted by them both over the next several months. Shell's strong reservations were left behind with the excuse that all the old societal rules were trite and outdated. She heard the warning bells sound off in her head when Len brought up the notion of moving in together just one month after their first dinner, but she stifled her instinct and said that maybe they could think it over. Len chose to take her muted reaction as a sign of complicity, and soon they were out on the weekends looking for rent houses in Oklahoma City, where Leonard had decided they would both find jobs after their May graduation.

Everything moved so quickly with Leonard at the helm of the ship, steering in the direction of his choosing. Shell felt like a passenger, never in agreement but never speaking up to protest either. Several times she was struck by the realization that someone should put on the brakes and soon. She made a few half-hearted efforts, but at the first sign of malcontent Len would direct the conversation in another direction and avoid the unpleasant subjects Shell had started to evoke. She knew it was cowardice that restrained her from dealing straight with Len, but still she sat back and let him charge ahead rather than deal with the ugly facts. He took her reticence as a sign of agreement and in truth he did not care to know if she felt otherwise. As long as Shell was with him and he was not alone he was satisfied.

The trouble now, all this time later, was that Shell was finally starting to send out the warning signals she should have done long before. They came as an unwelcome interference, since Len's plans were already rearranged, the move back to Boston was abandoned and the future was dead set around their relationship.

Now, as they drove on toward the Oklahoma border he found himself in a near panic. The stories she laughed at in the past only made her eyes roll now. Shell was drifting away and he had to get her back. Shell loved him, he was sure of it, and now he had this one chance embodied in a weekend roadtrip to turn it all around. He knew just what had to be done.

Chapter 5

Shell

> *It's so easy to blow up your problems.*
> *It's so easy to play up your breakdown.*
> The Cars, "Moving in Stereo"

The little car and its silent double occupants put two hours and a couple hundred miles between themselves and the cement compound of the city. The interstate was a repetitive reel of median and trees with an occasional exit off to the insular world of a sleeping small town.

Leonard and Shell drove past several exits before deciding to stop for fuel in a little town called Lyman that was little more than an hour away from their destination for the night. The needle on the gas gauge dipped down and just touched the top of the empty red zone. Plus, Shell had to pee. The car followed the exit ramp to a two-lane state highway that ran right through the middle of the town. They drove past the darkened outlines of a curiosity shop and a dusty old diner that had not served up a hot breakfast in thirty years. The place looked like a hospice patient on a slow starvation diet. Both Len and Shell noted the eerie emptiness of the town. Up ahead hunched a dull gas station, marked by a lighted yellow and white sign. Though a few bulbs were burned out on one side, it still shone out to travelers in the dusk like a garish beacon.

"I don't know if I want to use the bathroom in that place. Look at it," Shell said.

The exterior of the store had once been painted white, but it was now dulled by time and weather. The trash can that sat next to the entrance bulged from the overflow and had not been emptied in days. Food wrappers, receipts, and half empty Styrofoam cups littered the sidewalk.

"This is the only stop I'm making, Shell. Put some toilet paper down on the seat and get after it. Or else pee in a cup." Len chuckled at the thought and stepped outside. He grabbed the handle of the gas pump and walked to the rear of the car. Shell flipped down the visor and made a quick mirror check. Just in the past couple of months she noticed her face had aged. *I'm getting old*, she thought to herself, *lined like a book*. She flipped the mirror back into place and got out of the car.

She made her way across the oil-slicked parking lot and walked through the entrance of the convenience store. She made a point to avoid eye contact with the clerk, though she felt certain he had an eye on her while she walked toward the back of the store to find the toilets. A cardboard sign taped to the wall beside a dented metal door signaled the bathroom. Shell pulled up the bottom of her shirt, wrapped it around her hand and used it to turn the grey metal handle. She was no clean freak but she had a hunch the place had not been scrubbed down in some time. She took a step into the dimly-lit room, and the reeking smell of ammonia and chlorine assaulted her nostrils. The large square tiles on the floor curved downward one after another to accommodate a drain located in the floor of the stall. *Why is a drain in the floor*, she wondered, *if there isn't a shower in here?* An ancient towel dispenser hung on the wall near the door.

SHELL

Shell hurried into the stall and decided she would need to rely on mind over matter in order to accomplish her urinary task. The wall behind the stool had been knocked in at some point, perhaps to access the plumbing behind. She could see the curved old pipes worming around behind what looked to be a small piece of cardboard in the open space back there. The toilet itself was ringed with brown stains as if it had not been cleaned since installation. Still, she had to go, and there was no chance she could make it to the next town–even if Len could be convinced to stop.

She steeled herself and turned to face away from the toilet. Her hands met at her midsection and unbuttoned her pants. She unzipped and pushed her jeans and panties down to her ankles in one motion and scooted her feet backward an inch at a time so as not to trip. When she was as close to the toilet as she dared go, she bent her torso at the waist and leaned forward, squatting down, lowering her haunches to within just a few inches of the toilet seat, hands placed squarely across her thighs to support her weight.

The pressure on her bladder released and she could feel tiny little splashes of water and urine flecking the back of her legs. She grimaced. *I'd rather pee myself than touch any of the shit-stained porcelain in this place,* she thought. She just wanted to get her business done and get out of there. She contracted and pushed on her stomach muscles to move the water out in haste.

She thought about the hole in the wall and felt the sudden sensation she was being watched. She clenched herself and stood up quickly, jerking up her pants as she turned to look back at the hole in the wall. She couldn't know for sure, but thought she saw a tiny flash of light in the hollowed wall. The flash went dark in an instant and she did not know whether her eyes could be trusted or if her imagination was in high gear set off by the creepy surroundings.

She buttoned her jeans, kicked a foot up on the handle and pushed it down. Water ran from the toilet handle, down the foggy silver pipe and into the stool. It was discolored and combined with Shell's urine to make a small rust-colored pool swirling there in the streaked bowl. She waited a moment and realized with alarm that the rancid water was rising beyond the normal mark. Here was the reason for the drain in the floor. She was at a full-tilt when she burst from the bathroom. Even as she walked out she had decided not to say anything to Len. He had already decided she was losing it after the incident at home with that weird bird.

The clerk was still in the same spot behind his register, but now he wore a bit of a queer smirk on his face. Shell's cheeks were flushed with anger and embarrassment. Her brown eyes sparked.

"I'm sure you're aware of the state of that bathroom?" She asked the cashier. She squared her shoulders as she spoke and met his eyes so he would know she was serious.

"What? Out of toilet paper or somethin', Miss?" He wore a name tag that read Eugene. His toothless smirk grew wider and the thin skin of his hollow cheeks crinkled up in thin rolls of skin. A scraggled growth of beard grew in little patches here and there across his gaunt face.

"That is far from the worst of it," she said in a businesslike manner. "I'd like to speak to the manager, please."

"This place belongs to me, Sugar. So I guess you'll just have to settle for tellin' *ME* what troubles you so damn much." He grinned down at her, his gums wet and slimy with tobacco juice. "You can bet I'll fix you right up," he said, sneering. "This *IS* a FULL. SERVICE. STATION. young lady. Come on, tell me what you *NEED!*" He said, shoving his pelvis forward and grabbing at his package. "You got a HOLE that needs pluggin'? I'll check your oil too! *Ooo wee*, that oughta be good and messy! Reckon you're the kinda woman keeps her oil changed regular? No? Well how about we check *all* your fluids? Maybe that's your problem. You're all *dried up*, lady!"

Shell's hand rose involuntarily to cover her mouth. Shock cemented her feet in place for the moment. The cashier's hand remained on his crotch bouncing up and down, up and down, his shoulders leaned back, eyebrows arched toward his scalp line in anticipation. He was having a blast.

"I, I…" she stuttered and her face turned another shade of red entirely.

"*I…I…I…*" he parroted back, mocking. Thin strings of spittle strung across the cavern of his mouth while he dropped his chin and repeated the word *I*.

"I'm going to get my husband!" She shrieked, ecstatic that she was at least able to force a few words out of her mouth, however ridiculous they may have been. She had no idea why she referred to Len as her "husband." Maybe the word carried more weight in her mind than the word "boyfriend." Shell dropped her hand from her mouth and made for the door at the same time. The heels of her boots left little half-moon circles on the dirty floor behind her. She stormed outside and hoped that Eugene was scared to death—or at least as disturbed as she had been.

Len had long since finished pumping the gas and was sitting in the driver's seat with his head down, checking messages on his phone. Shell loped across the fifty yards from the store to the gas pumps and slammed her palm on his window.

Len jumped in his seat and snapped the phone down on the console. He turned the key one click forward in the ignition so he could roll down the window. Shell began to blurt a river of words before Len had a chance to ask what the matter was.

"That guy in there just harassed me, Len! Oh my God, you wouldn't believe the things he said. I came out of the restroom and it was so filthy I almost threw up and I don't know for sure, but I think someone was in there peeking through a hole in the wall and then when I came out that guy said the most awful things, Len, are you hearing me? Do something, please!"

"Slow down, Shell, are you serious?"

"You know I wouldn't make a joke about something like that," she cried. "Please go and do something about it!"

"What the hell do you want *me* to do? Go in there and get myself shot in this Podunk-BFE, where the only cop in town is probably that guy's first–"

He stopped mid-sentence and looked past Shell. The faint tinkling of the bell hanging over the gas station's door sounded. Shell became very still because she knew, without looking, that the cashier was walking toward the car. There could make no mistake in pairing Len's expression and the sound of that little bell.

"Get out of the way, Shell." Len grabbed her arm and slid her out of the way. He opened the door and stepped out, positioning himself and the door between the cashier and Shell. She was relieved and more than a little surprised. He had never done anything like that to protect her before.

Eugene walked right up to Len. He never looked at Shell and did not appear to be frightened in the least.

"What's going on here?" Len asked. He threw his shoulders back and bowed out his chest at the man's approach. He looked a little like a puffed up banty rooster. Shell noted that he spoke in a much deeper voice than usual.

"Well, sir, I just wanted to tell you good folks not to worry a spot about what happened back there in the toilet. I could tell your missus there was real embarrassed and upset when she came out of the john and I just want y'all to know it ain't no big deal. Why, it just kind of goes along with the business. For some reason or th'other people traveling for long ways over the road sometimes get their bowels all worked up and runny. H'aint no other choice but to stop in here and relieve yourself. No other exits or restrooms for twenty miles or so in either direction. Why, I figure there's at least five other people stopped in here over the past month with the runnin' off themselves. I mean *bad* diarrhea. Why, that mess your lady left in there ain't nothin' in comparison, to tell you the truth."

"What? Uh, sir... Look, I'm sorry—" Len looked down and read Eugene's name tag. "I'm sorry, Eugene; my girlfriend just told me you harassed her. Now *listen*: if that's the case we're going to have to file a police report."

Eugene looked over Len's head and met Shell's eyes for a micro-second, just to let her know he had registered the lie she'd told about having a husband. She looked down at the dirty cement and he returned his attention to Len.

"Oh, I'm truly sorry for that misunderstandin'. That's why I come out here was to clear things up. I knew I upset her but that shore wunt what I was meanin' to do. I must've embarrassed her asking about that toilet in there. It was overflowin' after she come out, and I was just trying to figger out what she'd flushed down in there. Just wanted to make sure she didn't flush no tampax or nothin' of the like down that stool. Wimmin do that a lot you know; I just don't think they have a clue about what that does to the plumbin'. Those girl plugs, why, they get stuck up in there and, boy, they'll just swell up like an ole balloon. Stops her up right quick; not a drop of water'll get through. You have to excuse me sir; we don't come across too many classy women in here. Mostly just a bunch a lot lizards and whores."

Len turned and looked over his shoulder at Shell. He widened his eyes in disbelief and a bit of wicked amusement.

"Um, Shell, how about we just let this go, okay? The man said he was sorry."

"He's a *liar!*" she hissed at Len. "You should have heard what he said. Said he'd plug my *hole*, or something like that."

"Oh my goodness, ma'am," Eugene interjected, looking past Len with a gleam in his eye. Len mistook the shine as a tear of genuine regret rather than delighted amusement.

"Now listen here," said Eugene. "You misunderstood me. Gosh, I hate that you think I'd say things like that to a customer. What I was tryin' to ask was whether the hole in the bathroom was plugged up. I just needed to know if that ole toilet was stopped up and overflowin' again. I guess you was so upset you misunderstood."

"You know what," said Len. "We're in a hurry, and we just don't have time for this. Don't worry about it, sir. We'll get going." "Just get in the car, Shell."

"Get going? You're going to take this guy's word over mine?"

"Shut up, Shell," he said through clenched teeth. "Let's just get out of here."

Resigned, she walked around behind the back of the car to the passenger door. Once inside, she reached over and locked the door before pulling the seat belt across her midsection and locking it into the buckle.

She heard the muffled voices of Len and the man exchanging a few more words outside the car. The sound of the conversation was too soft for her to make out the words, but Len's tone was much lighter now, and the tension seemed to have lifted. She thought of explaining the entire incident to Len when he got back into the car and then decided against it. Too late now to do anything. She knew what had happened, but maybe Len was right. If there were an officer in the town, he or she probably would have laughed at the two of them marching in to demand a police report because Uncle Eugene made a joke out of some snotty city lady again. Nothing more could be done now, short of taking Len into that filthy restroom to see the hole in the wall for himself. Shell could not bear the thought of it.

She made a promise to herself to call the local police station after the weekend was over anyway, so she could report the guy and the hole in the bathroom wall. Maybe she would just call the highway patrol. *For now*, she told herself, *the best way to avoid any more trouble is to get on home and as far away from this godforsaken place as possible.*

Len opened the car door and heaved a deep sigh when he got himself behind the wheel and shut the door.

"What in hell was *that*, anyway? Could you believe that freak? Straight out of *Deliverance*, I'm telling you! I kept expecting him to say, 'Squeal like a pig, boy!'" Len let out another great whoosh of air, as though he had just triumphed after some great personal challenge. He chuckled to himself, started the engine, and turned the wheels to steer out of the parking lot.

Shell looked back over her right shoulder as the car veered off toward the road. Old Eugene was standing just inside the store's doorway, a rotten smart-assed smile plastered from ear to ear. Shell raised her fist up to the window and unleashed her middle finger at him. In return, Eugene raised two fingers to his mouth in a V and flicked his tongue in and out. Len didn't see the gesture, and Shell didn't tell him about it. Their little weekend jaunt was already stranger than she ever imagined, and things were just getting started.

Len drove on without remarking further about Shell's run-in with the cashier. In truth, he was embarrassed. He had no doubt that the dumb hillbilly freak had gotten out of line, and he wished he had been the kind of guy that would walk right up and clock a man on the chin. But he was not that kind of man. His father had reminded him of that fact almost every day of his childhood for as long as he could remember. His own father had called him a sissy with regularity. No matter what he did to try and prove himself, he was always a sissy. The toothless grin the guy had flashed at them made Len sick to his stomach and brought back the worst memory he had of his father. Shell was always bitching, asking why he didn't leave to go back and see his father, but she did not understand the kind of man his father was. Not the type for a pleasant visit. Not at all.

Leonard couldn't have been more than eight the first time his father called him a sissy. He had been playing in the living room of his family home when he heard an unfamiliar sound coming from the kitchen. It was a strange crunching and popping sound, as though someone were in there snapping candy canes. He set his little red Tonka car back into its case with care and stood, walking quietly toward the kitchen. He was able to stay silent with the help of his little footed pajamas. That sound kept coming louder—the grinding and the cracking. He stopped just at the entryway, keeping his body in the living room and only allowing the top portion of his head to turn the corner and peer into the kitchen.

There stood his father at the sink with his massive back to him. Len was immediately frightened. He had received countless beatings from his father: sometimes because he had done something wrong; sometimes just because his father had too much to drink. Though Len knew his mother loved him, she was powerless when his father tied one on. The only other sound to register besides his own pleas for help was the sound of his poor mother crying behind the locked door of her bedroom. She wasn't home that day in the kitchen, and he knew, even at the age of eight, that her absence made his own situation all the more dangerous.

He stood there still for several minutes, peering into the kitchen at his father's back and trying to put together in his young mind what was happening at the sink. He could see that his father was doing something with his hands. He had his head bent down. Len heard that cracking sound again, and this time he heard a very low, guttural groan. That did it; even though he may have been scared of his dad, he loved him nonetheless and that sound meant he must be hurt. Len rushed across the kitchen floor to his father's side.

The sink was a bloody mess. Several small whitish things were scattered around in the silver sink. Blood pooled around them and ran in small streams down into the drain. None of this made sense to Len, but he was instantly seized with terror. His line of sight followed the stream of blood from the sink up to his father's mouth and a sight that was horrific beyond the comprehension of an eight-year-old boy.

His father stood with a large tool in both hands. Len had seen him use it many times, tightening bolts on the machinery around their house. From this vantage point, they appeared almost serpent-like. His father had called them Channellocks. They were joint pliers, the kind of pliers that had a sliding lower jaw needed for a strong clamp. The bottom jaw could be adjusted to grasp onto something as large as a gas nozzle. Or something as small as a tooth. The serrated teeth on the jaws of the pliers held fast. Leonard's father was prying out his own teeth.

He looked down at Len and gave a little grin at his son. He had already removed three of his front teeth. Len looked up and saw the dark red slushy holes from which blood poured out in ribbons. The sight made him think of the raw hamburger meat his mother sometimes left out on the counter to thaw for dinner. He could smell the alcohol emanating from his father's pores. Now that he was up close, he could see that his dad was wobbling back and forth on the balls of his feet.

Len did not know how where his strength came from, but he somehow managed to speak. "Dad, ah… Are you okay?" Tears were streaming down his face because he was sure now that nothing was okay. Something terrible was happening to his dad; something awful that made his father hurt himself, and Leonard knew he was too small to make it stop.

"I had a toothache," his father slurred, and began to laugh. It was a horrible, insane sound that held no love or humor. The laugh was empty. As he spoke, a spray of blood erupted from the dark cavity of his mouth and landed on his young son's face. Len reached up and felt the wetness on his cheek.

His father stopped laughing and reached up again with the Channellocks to grab hold of the elongated and yellowed incisor tooth. He braced his feet against the counter and leaned forward over the edge of the sink. With a strong, rapid motion he pushed the handles straight out into the air in front of his mouth and then came that awful sound again; that cracking noise that had first caught Len's attention. The sound of the roots breaking off inside his father's gums.

The tooth did not come out yet. He reversed the head of the Channelocks now, so that the head was pointing inside his mouth, and ratcheted it in the same direction from whence it had come. He pushed both the tool and the tooth backward into his mouth and then pulled it forward again, until he was sure the tooth was broken at the roots in the front and the back. At last he pulled the tool downward and out it came, with a sickening suction sound as the gums released their quarry and tiny pieces of bright red flesh fell out into the sink along with copious amount of blood. His father opened up the handles of the tool, and out fell the incisor with a tiny clink next to the other three teeth that lay there haphazard.

Len was sure his father would die. He had never seen so much blood. He hadn't known a human body held that much. He knew that if he dialed for the police or an ambulance, his father would beat him to death before a savior arrived. He began to sob. As he turned and ran away, his father called after him, "you get back here, *sissy*, I'm gonna pull your teeth!"

Little Leonard Harris ran through the living room and down the hall to his bedroom. He threw himself under the bed and pulled a pillow over his head to drown out the muffled cracking and popping. For the rest of his life, and no matter what anyone ever said to the contrary, Len knew that monsters were real and sometimes they lived in your own kitchen.

Chapter 6

Rachel

> *For only love can conquer hate;*
> *you know we've got to find a way.*
> Marvin Gaye, "What's Goin' On"

Rachel considered the implausible events that plagued the Cherokee migration mile after burdened mile. When the journey first began, she'd been able to find fleeting solace by picturing their old home in her mind. She imagined the trees. They would be stark and leafless by now, barely moving in the winter wind. She remembered the rattled sound of dead leaves swirling and tumbling at her feet. She remembered, though they were always just beyond her reach, the gray stones her father set out in the pathway to their front door. But now, after more than a month on the trail and even with her eyes squeezed tight, the image of their old home would not come back. Perhaps it was the mind's way of neatly disposing of things that would never again manifest themselves in reality; the distinct memory of such a heavy loss might only serve to wreak an unbearable emotional toll. With each step now, she had to try and force her imagination to picture a new and better land ahead: a place where her family could find a fertile field in a river valley, perhaps. It would be a place to sow their seeds and see a blessed yield for all.

A bitter cold front had blown in from the north, and a great fear circulated through their numbers. They worried that the passage across the Mississippi River would be frozen over. Sloan assured them the mighty river would not freeze completely; he had not seen such a thing in all the years he had travelled over it. But even the leader himself did not seem convinced of his own reassurances, which he delivered under shadow of a troubled brow. He knew the people had not yet seen the worst of their trials. Not even close. His fears were confirmed by a traveler riding back toward the east, away from the river.

"I'm telling you there's no use," the weary man warned Sloan. "The river's froze up solid. Won't be passable for weeks, and that's only if the wind changes direction and comes down from the south."

Despite the many miles that yet lay ahead, the proximity of the river heralded a cautious optimism in their ranks. The river was a milestone. A signpost for the last half of the trail. The news that it was frozen over shattered fragile hopes for deliverance. Abject despair overcame many. Representatives from each family gathered to discuss what would be done. Some wanted to stay until the thaw came. A few wanted to turn back, but for what, they could not say. At last, the decision was made that the people would continue on to the banks of the great river, and remain there until the thaw. Then they would be ready to move across at the first possible opportunity, rather than sit a day's journey away. Most agreed that the superior choice must be the one that would bring an end to their calamity as quickly as possible.

The ice was a solid sheet when they reached the river. The air temperature in the valley was ten degrees colder than up above, in the pasture lands. The people were forced to leave their oxen and cattle to forage on the frozen fields above, and themselves sought shelter in caves that the river had carved into the land thousands of years before.

Rachel and her family crowded into a cave with two other families. They lifted Mahala from the wagon, carried her down the slippery bank, and moved her back against the far wall of the cave. The air inside was frigid, but still warmer than the wild icy winds that howled up and down the Mississippi day and night.

William built fire after fire to fight the cold, using every scrap of firewood that could be retrieved from the barren terrain. When he saw that some families were unable to find enough firewood, he shared as much as he could spare while still keeping his family alive through the night. The days were intolerable while the cold snap lasted, but the nights were torturous. With every morning came the light of day, but the warmth of the sun was hidden by thick cloud cover. Their hope of a river crossing hung along with it.

Rachel secretly felt that the weather's delay must have been Yowa's way to ensure her reunion with Major. For the first day, she scarcely registered the intensity of the freezing cold. She kept peering out toward the edge of the river valley in hopes she might see him riding toward them with more food and medicine. But her daydreams of rescue did not last long, as she watched more people dying, frozen in the caves that surrounded them.

At night, all four of the Reeses depended on the body heat generated each other to stay alive. William and Ani were at nearest the mouth of the cave, next to Mahala. Rachel lay on the other side of her grandmother. No one spoke of it, but they were all aware that Mahala's survival depended on the ability of the rest to provide her with warmth. Her health declined again, along with the temperature. At night, when Rachel turned her back to the night air and willed the warmth in her body over to her grandmother, she would place her hand on Mahala's arm and pray they would be delivered from the frozen purgatory. Her grandmother's emaciated upper arm had once been soft and warm, but now it was colorless and cold.

On the sixth night in the cave, the family huddled against each other as they had every night before, but this time Mahala reached out to grip Rachel's arm. Rachel said nothing, but turned her head so that her cheek was on the hard stone floor and her eyes looked directly into her grandmother's. They were speaking now, but there were no words. Mahala told Rachel that the time had come to join their ancestors. The glittery life-light left her eyes, and Rachel felt Mahala's spirit leave. It was the only warmth she'd felt in weeks. Mahala's spirit travelled seamlessly away from her body and was gone.

The next morning, the sun came up and the thaw began with the first few drips of ice releasing itself back into water. No sense of hope came with the thaw, only the weary realization that it was time to move again. The ground was hard and refused to accept their dead into its soil. As the ice on the river broke apart, streams of water ran down over the hanging rocks. All of the drops taken together could not match the gathering of tears that streamed from the eyes of the Cherokee. The salt and water fell from their faces and dropped to the ground, mixing with the snow and the soil. For a hundred years to come, their bones would be found along the trails and the caves that ran, like their bloodlines, from Georgia to Indian Territory.

Rachel knelt over her grandmother with Ani by her side. William stood at the mouth of the cavern, chanting the songs of their ancestors. They wrapped Mahala's precious face with strips of cloth and washed her body clean with pure water from the fresh snow melt. The preparation of her body meant they would be among the last of the people to leave the camp. Rachel placed her hand over Mahala's heart and murmured a prayer to ask that Yowa accept the soul of her loved one so that she would be made strong and whole once again. She asked once more that her people who still remained on the earth might be delivered to their new homeland, if Yowa's will would be served by their survival.

Rachel became numb at the absence of Major and the departure of Mahala. She wondered how the long enduring presence of her grandmother could be so quickly gone, and marveled that the vibrant hope that filled her for Major's arrival had left as well. She felt foolish to have trusted the man with her heart; it was the least among her possessions but the most vital to her existence. Ani recognized despair in the shadow of her daughter's face but was unable to counsel her out of her sorrow as she had always done in the past. Ani understood that for innocents the loss of life and love left fresh cut wounds that brought greater pain because it was not expected. The young had no scars to protect them.

William had no time to consider the heavy toll paid by his daughter. He too was numb to his surroundings. He was concerned with remaining alive and sane. He allowed himself to focus on one thought alone: he had to bring his wife and daughter to the end of the trail alive. If he could accomplish this one thing—if he could summon the strength to make it—then surely any trials in the new territory could be managed. He would have to grieve the death of his mother after he saw that Ani and Rachel were safe. He swore an oath that he would not allow another member of his family to be lost to the trail.

The three sat together, waiting to board the ferry in order to cross over the river. Three white puffs of frozen air expelled from each of their mouths and disappeared into the air. Ani was grateful that William was quiet now and at her side. The ferryman had demanded fifty dollars to take them across, knowing full well they would have to pay any price he named. William was infuriated, but within the course of a few seconds Ani watched him reign in his anger. She swallowed the pain of witnessing her husband's defeat. He nodded at Ani to hand the last of their money over. The ferryman accepted the payment and hastily stuck the bills into his shirt pocket, then rushed off to release the ferry from its moorings. He noted the murder in William's eyes and knew that he should hurry this particular group of Indians over to the western bank and off of his boat. The Reese family shared a blanket and stood in a half-circle, eyes fixed upon the west and the fate that awaited them.

Chapter 7

Shell

> *Listen real close to me baby: you just wait and see, lady.*
> Leon Russell, "Lady Blue"

Shell was relieved when they drove across the bridge spanning the Illinois River. She was almost home. Home. Safe. She rolled down the window and stuck her head out to take in a deep breath of heavy river air. The smell was organic and familiar; one of rich soil, rain, and vegetation. She wanted to be immersed in it.

"We're almost there!" She said.

The sound of excitement returned to her voice for the first time since she'd heard the Leon Russell tune earlier in the day. The sun had already dipped below the tree line in the sky behind them, but she didn't need the benefit of light to take in the scenery outside. This place in the Ozark foothills was emblazoned on her brain. The landscape was most striking in late fall, when the maple and oak trees provided a patchwork quilt of scarlet and orange across the hills.

"Ah, I'm beat," Len said. "I'm going to bed as soon as we get there."

"Surely you'll stay up and visit with my family for at least a little while? It would be so rude to go straight to bed. They've been waiting on us."

"I thought you told them not to wait up."

"Well, I did, but I know they will anyway. It's just the way they are."

"I'll stay up long enough to have a beer, then I'm going to bed."

"Okay, that's fair enough."

Len slowed the car and turned off the highway. The wheels hit the gravel road of the Foster driveway. Sure enough, they could see lights glowing inside the front room of the house.

"See, I told you they'd still be up," Shell said. Len rolled his eyes with great animation, knowing that Shell would not notice in the dark. He lacked appreciation for the big family reunion scene that he knew was coming. He found the Fosters loud, obnoxious, and just a tad false. Within twenty-four hours the new sheen would wear off, and they would all begin to annoy each other. The façade would roll back from all the unnecessary enthusiasm, and it would be time to leave again. He preferred to have things that way: just him and Shell.

The car came to a stop in the driveway. Before Len could turn off the engine, the front door swung open and the large silhouette of Shell's dad came into view. He lit up a cigarette and took a deep drag. The end of it burned with a tiny orange glow. He walked out onto the porch with a wide smile spanning his weathered face.

"Get in here!" Dean Foster yelled.

"Go on in and see your family," Len said to Shell. "I'll get the bags."

He didn't have to say it twice. She jumped out of the car and ran across the lawn to hug her father.

"I didn't think you'd ever get here," he exclaimed. "What happened?"

Shell laughed a little. "You wouldn't believe me if I told you, Dad."

"Let's go in and you can give it a whirl," he replied.

She walked in and found that her mother had also waited out their arrival, passing the time in the kitchen baking Shell's favorite—fresh banana bread. Shell walked straight to the bar and grabbed a piece.

"Oh, don't use your fingers, Shell. At least have the common decency to get a plate and fork." She turned toward the words floating up the hall to see her mother, Christie Foster, approaching with a twinkle in her eye. Shell felt for a moment that she was watching an older version of her own self walk in.

"Don't start nagging already, Mom," she said. "I haven't even had the chance to sit down yet!" Shell stepped forward and wrapped her arms around her mother's shoulders as she spoke.

Just behind Christie came Jennifer. She wore pink-footed pajamas with her hair pulled up in a ponytail that sat directly on top of her head. In this get-up Jenny looked like she might still be twelve years old instead of twenty-five, and Shell found it impossible to restrain her laughter.

"What's so funny?" her sister said, bobbing her head up and down and waving a finger in Shell's face. They all enjoyed a good joke, but Jenny was by far the most animated.

Shell gave Jennifer a hug and took a seat on the couch after embracing her sister. She decided to spare them the disturbing details of the journey and instead launched the conversation right away into the topic of the next day's destination.

"Dad, do you remember back when Jenny and I were kids, a long time ago, when you told us the story of the Hornet Spooklight?"

Dean Foster held his glasses in one hand and the bottom of his nightshirt in the other, trying to polish off the smudges that had been left there by Shell's hug. He paused for a couple of seconds without looking up and then slowly began rubbing the shirt in circles on the lenses.

"I know the story—but I don't remember the particulars of telling you about it," he said, looking up from his work at last. "Why do you ask?"

Shell was not surprised that her father failed to remember that night on the river. He had been a heavy drinker through much of her childhood. Fifteen years later, his passionate affection for booze was replaced by an equally addicting love for old-time religion. He'd made a dramatic recovery just about the time Shell left home for college. Dean Foster's timing was also just in time to keep Christie from filing for a divorce. Everyone agreed that only divine intervention had kept him alive and the marriage intact.

Shell's recollection was interrupted when the door flung open and in walked Leonard, dragging her suitcase behind him, the strap of his overnight bag slung across his shoulder. The door stop was broken, so the door swung fully open and the handle hit the wall. It left a slight impression in the beige paint.

"Len, buddy! I'm sorry I didn't come out to help you unload." Dean apologized. "To tell you the truth, we just got caught up talking about your big road trip tomorrow."

"Dad, don't worry about it; he told me he'd get the bags," Shell said, though she did not sound convinced at all. Her gaze followed Len across the room. She hoped he would not make a scene already, right here in front of her parents.

Len acted as though he did not hear the words spoken in his direction and continued to drag the bags across the living room, red faced. Dean rose from his recliner and walked over to try and take one of the bags from him. When he reached a hand to Len's shoulder, Len swiped out and knocked back Dean's outstretched hand. The room's occupants took in a collective gasp. Shell's father was slow to anger, but once his temper was triggered few could contain him.

"Len!" Shell shouted in dismay.

"Do you have a clue how much these goddam bags weigh, any of you?" he asked in an accusatory tone. He directed the words and spite toward Shell and avoided eye contact with the rest. As far as he was concerned, they could all hang. Every last fat-assed one of them. He walked past their shocked faces and carried on down the hall to the guest room, bouncing the wheeled suitcase on the hardwood floor to emphasize his disgust.

"Oh God, you guys; I'm so sorry, he's been in such a terrible mood lately. Dad—I don't know what to say…" She looked to her father. He was unable to mask his anger.

"Oh sister, don't worry about it," he said, delivering the words through clenched teeth. "I should have had the presence of mind to go help him."

The occupants of the room were held hostage by an awkward silence.

"Forget about it," Jenny broke in. "Len's just tired, so let him sleep. Jeez, what an asshole." Shell laughed, more from her own relief at a break in the tension than at her sister's words.

Never one to tolerate a serious mood for long, Jennifer moved on: "Now, what *were* we talking about?"

"I'm going to try and find the Spooklight tomorrow," said Shell. "You told us about it a long time ago, Dad. When we were little girls. It's the main reason I came down this weekend."

"You know, I haven't thought about that in so long," her father replied. His voice trailed off as though he spoke to himself instead of to the others.

Shell was just pleased to have shifted her father's attention away from Len. Any other topic would do as far as she was concerned.

"I'll tell you this," her father said. "You shouldn't set out looking for something like that; something supernatural that isn't at rest. Nobody knows what it is, of course, but I'll tell you what it isn't: it isn't of God."

Shell winced and hoped her father did not notice. She wanted to avoid the fire and brimstone, this-sinful-world-is-coming-to-a-fiery-end kind of wretched conversation that was commonplace since her father had given up the bottle and taken up the Bible. She didn't have anything against his newly strengthened faith. She was happy he'd found some peace. But she also felt a little awkward in discussion, the subject too intimate for debate.

She considered herself a Christian too, albeit an inherited one, kind of like the Jewish people. She didn't study the Bible or talk to God, but her family had always been Christian. She happened to enjoy life for the most part and found the apocalyptic part of the whole story dour and depressing. She didn't see any reason to focus on that one part of the message. So, as with most topics she found unpleasant, she avoided religious discussion wherever possible.

Her father had gotten up to rummage through a dark wicker bin full of books he kept beneath a coffee table next to the couch. He pulled out a well-worn Bible, held together at the spine with frayed duct tape.

He opened it with care and flipped through before stopping and turning a few pages slowly and with great deliberation. "Here," he said. "Here it is, Second Corinthians. 'Even Satan disguises himself as an angel of light.'" He looked up as though waiting for her to reply. "Straight from the word of God," he said.

Shell took a deep breath. "Okay, so let's assume I go there and find this thing, say it's real and some kind of supernatural light really *is* floating around up there…why do you have to make it out to be something bad? Why couldn't it be a good light?" She felt very strange contradicting her father. She disagreed with a multitude of his avowed views and politics, but she never said much to contradict him aloud. How silly she felt now, arguing with him over, of all things, a Spooklight. They might as well have been debating the Mothman.

"It's an eerie place up there, Shell. So many tragedies. You wouldn't believe all the horrible things that have gone on up at the border. Not just once or twice, but over and over again for hundreds of years. Some places in this world breed evil. It's bad earth. You can feel it when you go there. That sick feeling you get in the pit of your stomach? That isn't superstition. When you get that feeling, it's your brain telling you it's time to run." He leaned forward and demanded eye contact. "When you drive up there, before you ever get to Spooklight Road, you'll know in your gut you don't belong there."

"Tragedy?" She asked half-heartedly. She didn't want to listen anymore, but repeated the word back to him so he would know she was paying attention.

"Yes. The Cherokee don't mess around up there. I'm telling you. When you go, just look around; you'll see. It's a wasteland."

"They have a Quapaw *casino* up there, Dean," Christie Foster interrupted, laughing at her husband. "Have you lost your mind? No Indians!" she scoffed, shaking her head.

"Oh, they have a casino. And you can go inside and see plenty of natives working there. But they took their families and left a long time ago. They're still making money, sure. But as far as their homes—no way. They don't live anywhere close."

Shell had a difficult time believing Dean's story. Still, she humored him. "What happened to make them leave?"

"Land was ruined. Mining company tore it up. All the water's poisoned. No good."

"It can't be all bad."

"You'll see when you get there," Dean repeated. "I know I can't stop you from going. You always do just exactly what you want, no matter what anyone else tells you."

She shook her head in disagreement. She was amazed that her father took the Spooklight issue so seriously. The main reaction she'd expected from her family had been a little ridicule for driving so far to chase after out a silly old legend. But here he was, pining on and on over a ghost-light.

"Promise me one thing," he said.

"What's that?"

"If it's real—if you see a light—don't wait for it to get close. Just promise me you'll say '*I rebuke you in the name of Jesus Christ.*'"

Shell fought off a strong urge to roll her eyes straight back in her head. "Dad, come on," she said with a curt little nervous laugh. "Are you serious?"

She knew the answer, though, before she even asked him. Her father said nothing.

"Okay, okay," she said in an irreverent tone. "But we probably won't see a thing anyway." None of her plans seemed to be working out according to her own expectations.

※ ※ ※

Alone in the guest room, Len rolled the suitcase inside and slammed the door shut behind him in a rush. He sat down on the edge of the bed, shoulders slumped forward, hands in his lap. He felt slightly embarrassed at his behavior, but it had all been because of Shell. The only thing he wanted—all he ever asked for, really—was for Shell to treat him like he mattered.

Now he had to walk in and watch her fawn over these people who didn't really know her all that well anymore. At least, they didn't know her like he did. He was envious of the way she acted around them. She'd adored him like that once, too. Her eyes had told him so, more than her words. He missed the attention, the sex. She'd treated him like a king for a while. He knew that at one time, he'd been the most important thing in her world, and also knew that she could make him feel that way again if she only wanted to. That was the most frustrating thing, he supposed; knowing that their troubles could all be fixed if Shell would just stop being so stubborn.

Len lay back on the bed, crossed his legs at the ankles and stretched his arms backward to rest his head upon his hands. His eyes turned up to the ceiling, and he allowed himself to think back to the first few months of their relationship. He found he did that a lot lately. He remembered the way she used to treat him and how she always paid attention to anything he had to say. Recalling those times was a way to keep from giving in to the panicked, helpless feeling that came over him every time he thought about her leaving. He decided to distract himself with the book he'd brought along. He had barely turned a page before the door to the guest room swung open and Shell stood there in the doorway.

"Glad you're finally coming to bed," he told her. Guilt came rushing back at the sight of her. He knew there was no excuse for his actions toward her family. Right now, he just wanted Shell to come in and shut the door so they could be alone and talk. She could lie down next to him, and maybe he would tell her he was sorry.

"I'm going out with my sister to watch the stars," she said in a voice that was monotone and devoid of emotion. "Do you want to come with us?"

"What do you think?"

"Ok. I'll be back in later."

"Don't fall asleep on the couch again."

"I won't." She pulled a worn, cream colored blanket from the small closet in the room and draped it at the foot of the bed. "Just in case you get cold."

He said nothing, but stared up at her as she stood over him. She could tell that he was more grateful than he should be; she would have done this kindness for any stranger without another thought.

"Goodnight, Len."

She stepped into the hall and pulled the bedroom door shut behind her. Len said something just as she closed the empty space between them, but Shell could not make out the words. She walked away as though he had never spoken.

Her sister sat on the couch with two red sleeping bags and some old pillows. "Ready?"

Even before Shell and Jennifer were old enough to comprehend, hundreds of clear, black nights found them in the same spot out on the lawn, lying on their backs, staring up into the ink of the evening sky. By now they should have been experts on astronomy, connoisseurs of the constellations, with the names and locations of each distant star and their faded, winking hues of blue and white committed to memory. But each time the sisters went out to take their places beneath the firmament it was as if for the first time, and all memory and experience of the last was wiped clean away. The secrets of space and time unfolded in a recurring play before them, its glittered actors shifting and moving, putting on display an eternal creationist formula in repetition. But they perceived the sight only as it was, with new eyes each time and no expectations of knowledge revealed or ancient prophecy foretold. In that deep vastness there loomed no future or history to bind them. Nothing asked in return.

At the rounded edges of the horizon where sky and earth met, the tree line reached up and held the two together. Silhouettes of twisted old oaks bent this way and that, the curved hooks of branches stitching celestial fabric into place, haphazard but sure.

The warm air hung heavy with water, as it tended to be in the hollowed river valley. It settled itself on the upturned faces of the girls and reflected a bit of their own light back to the sky.

"What the hell is wrong with him?" Jenny whispered.

The two had barely lain down when she started in. She'd disliked Leonard from their first introduction, but then, she never approved of any love interest Shell ever brought home to meet the family.

"We fought before we left. He wanted sex and I didn't. You know how that goes." Shell felt obligated to explain away Len's dramatic behavior in the living room. She'd tired of the subject and felt no desire to entertain a discussion of any depth about her feelings for Len.

"Bullshit," Jenny pressed on. "What's going on with you two? You both act and look like a couple of caged animals. I've never seen you so tense. If I wasn't broke, I'd bounce a quarter off your ass right now."

Shell suddenly became conscious of her body. Though she was lying flat, the muscles in her back were taut as if prepared to jump at any second. She stuck out her chin to elongate her neck, and her vertebrae made faint popping sounds as they moved apart. How strange, she thought, that her tendons and muscles were bound and restrained with such force without her own conscious permission.

"You don't really want to talk about Len, do you?" she asked.

"I just want to know what's happening in your life," said Jenny. "That's all. If that means we have to talk about Len, then let's talk about Len."

Their words floated straight up into the air. Neither turned to look at the other as they spoke. Shell was grateful that she didn't have to make eye contact.

"You want a smoke?" Jennifer held out a pack of cigarettes and a lighter.

"That's how cops get the perps to talk."

Jennifer's laugh tumbled out over the tall grass. "Jeez, it's the cops," she said, incredulous. "You know, nobody really uses the word 'perp' except for characters on NCIS or whatever." The tiny glow of Shell's cigarette burned and faded in the dark. She welcomed the faint nicotine high and the night air combined in her lungs.

"I have to end it with him." Shell had spoken the idea aloud for the first time. Even she was surprised by how certain she sounded.

"I knew it had to be bad," said Jenny. "Why did you bring him all the way up here if you're just going to dump him?"

"I've known it for a long time, but I just haven't had the guts to do it."

"What are you afraid of? That he'll hurt you or something?"

"No, no, nothing like that. Not even close. For starters, he's not capable of hurting me. But there is something. I don't know. It's like a real desperation about him lately that makes me wonder if maybe he'd try to hurt himself.

"He's just so alone," she went on. "His only friends are *my* friends. I've tried to get him to go back to Boston to see his old friends—and his parents for God's sake, make a stronger connection with them or something, you know, at the very least just to take some of the pressure off of me. But he doesn't act like he's interested in any other relationship but ours. And I don't mean that in a good way. When we met, I thought everything he said was so interesting. All those stories he told; I thought he must have had a thousand friends. He seemed so strong and confident. But over time, all the stories fell away. I think it must have all been a charade. It's just so hard to accept that none of that was real. We've been together for three years now. If I admit that none of it was real, I have to face up to some pretty serious problems of my own, you know?"

"What do you mean none of it was real? You've met some of his friends, haven't you? You've seen pictures and spoken to his family over the phone."

"I don't mean to say he's a complete fraud. It's just that he's kind of the opposite of the person I thought he was in the beginning."

"So he didn't live up to your expectations? You know I never liked the guy from the beginning. I'd be happy if you walked in and told him to leave right now. But you're being a hypocrite,

Shell. People put up fronts when they first meet. You're guilty of that, just as much as he is. Think about it. You kept your house sparkling clean. I mean, you went out and bought a drawer full of new lingerie. You started trying to *cook*." They both laughed at that because Shell's incompetency at the stove was legendary. Jennifer continued, "now your laundry is piled up again, you're probably wearing the same granny panties you had on when you heard the first Alice in Chains album… and you sure as shit don't cook. You wanted him to think you were some kind of a sex-crazed Betty Crocker in the beginning, didn't you? Admit it! And what man wouldn't think he'd died and gone straight to heaven after that? You can't blame him for wanting to hold on to *that*, Shell."

"I know, I know. That's one of the reasons I haven't been able to tell him it's over. I *am* a hypocrite. I never set out to be, though. But I also know that if I don't fix this now, I'll have to live the rest of my life with someone who isn't right for me. I think he'd be satisfied if we ran off and got married tomorrow. He'd have what he wants, but I'd be saddled with regret. I'm not willing to do that just to avoid hurting his feelings."

"You're just making things worse." Jennifer said. "You need to be done with it now. When are you going to tell him?"

"Maybe when we get back home. After this weekend, I guess."

"God, that's even worse. He'll know you've had him on the hook the whole time."

"What the hell else am I supposed to do, Jennifer?" Shell's voice rose in distress. "Waltz right in there and yell, '*Rise and shine*, you sonofabitch, NOW GET THE HELL OUT!' I mean all jokes aside; I can't do it here, right now."

"The sooner, the better."

Jennifer's attention shifted with a change in the sky. "What's going on with the stars? Look!" She pointed toward the southern sky. The stars were beginning to twinkle. It wasn't the usual flicker of one or two dying lights, but an odd blinking—on and off like a chest full of dark jewels. Shell watched with wide eyes. It was a bewildering, incredible sight. Every point of light in the sky flashed and blinked against the inky backdrop.

"Have you ever seen anything like that before?" Jennifer exclaimed.

"No," said Shell, breathless. It was as though a million strands of colored Christmas lights had been set on random and tossed up on high.

"Something strange must be going on in the atmosphere."

Even in awe of that spectacular sight, Shell's mind was still anchored in the nasty business that lay ahead with Len. The thought of it filled her with dread. She crossed her arms against her chest and felt tiny bumps set out a trail of gooseflesh over her skin, though not a breath of wind stirred.

She took in another deep breath and exhaled. "I'll do it tomorrow," she said to the sky. As she spoke the words up in the air the twinkling lights concluded their show and disappeared.

Chapter 8

Rachel

> *My mother said, to get things done,*
> *you better not mess with Major Tom.*
> David Bowie, "Ashes to Ashes"

Thomas Major's troubles began in town. The speed with which he packed his belongings surprised him. The entire lot fit easily within the fifteen-by-eight-foot space of the wagon bed. This came as a complete shock to him. He prided himself on a Spartan lifestyle but never realized until now how few material things he truly required. His house waited empty and clear as he stood in the doorway looking into its barren rooms. He felt no sense of sadness or sentimentality at the thought of leaving everything behind. This place was just a configuration of wood and steel and dirt; a marriage of material and geometry that bore out a man's shelter.

After the loss of his parents, Major had been plagued by the feeling that this place was not a real home. These perishables in all of their grand summation did not amount to much. Even now, with his life packed up and waiting in a wheeled box, he envisioned the ultimate destiny for this little house. The cedar boards would give way. The shingles above on the roof, so painstakingly aligned and sealed, would one day leak and begin to sag. They would succumb to a tiny drop of rain falling from above. The only certainty was in knowing the building would someday fall. And so it would be for all the rest. He would not wait here to watch the inevitable when he had at last discovered the one thing he knew would never fail him.

Rachel would never lose her spirit or her beauty. She was the reason for his newfound disdain for the trivial nature of earthly possessions. A new life was found in her, a new family. With Rachel, he found a deliverance that could save him. He'd been wandering in the wilderness and, until he'd found her, he'd never even realized he was lost. The thought of her sent a shiver through his body. For a moment, the hair on his arms stood on end. The physical effects he felt at the mere thought of her radiated to his very core. Rachel may as well have been classified a traveler from another world, because in his life no other human could match the effect she had on him, even in her absence.

Major leaned through the doorway and took one last look at the place. He felt a hitch in his chest at the thought of his mother and father. If they hadn't died so damned early, they would be here to see the miracle he had found.

He pictured two little brown-skinned babies, their chubby legs running through deep green grass, trailed by peals of bubbly laughter on a sweet summer breeze. The vision was as clear as any dream he'd ever had, and he felt like a glimpse of his own fate. With Rachel, he would have a family again. This was a vision of the future from God and had always been more than Major dared hope for. Maybe his mother would see her grandchildren from heaven. She would be so proud.

He was both comforted and driven by these thoughts. He kicked a small stone and watched it skid over the floor until it struck the far wall of the front room. "So long," he said to the stone and slammed the door behind him. He slung his overcoat across his shoulder. It was his fond farewell to a past that held no meaning. Life until now was a shiftless waste, and he was haunted by the notion that he might have spent the rest of his days there, satisfied and complacent, without Rachel at his side.

The team of horses observed their master's strange behavior with cool patience. They were a tall and muscular pair, bridled with a heavy tack and ready to work. Major felt pity as he looked at the fine sight of them, for they could not imagine the challenge of this next difficult journey. It would no doubt push both man and beast to their ultimate physical limits. The team startled and stamped their hooves when Major slammed the front door. Their heads remained facing forward, but their ears were turned in Major's direction.

A tall gentleman covered in a long brown coat wearing his finest hat, Major struck a handsome figure. He sat upright and proud in the buck seat as he urged the team onward in the direction of Golconda. It would be his one and only stop before he set out after Rachel. She had gone with her people nearly five days before. He was not worried about having fallen behind, because their progress would be slow with so many people in the treacherous winter conditions. He was sure he would catch them. Still, on a five hundred mile journey over wild terrain there were no safe wagers, and he did not want to waste another second.

Catching the group before they crossed the Mississippi was most important. There he would overtake them with another load of supplies, food, and medicine. He would help Rachel's family through the final leg of the long march and into Indian Territory. Then they would know he deserved their daughter's heart. He urged the team to a faster gait, anxious to get started.

The distance to town was only a few miles from his farm, and he could see its drab outline in contrast to the crisp white sky. The hue was a reflective bright white, as if to signify the shedding of this old life for one that would be perfect and new. He tilted his head down and shielded his eyes from the powerful reflection.

At a half mile's distance from town, Major saw a lone rider approaching. He was friendly with almost all the families in town, and the ones he didn't know only ever said he was a fine man. He was confident that no trouble would come.

He removed his hat and gestured with both hands in the air. The rider pulled back on his reigns and Major saw that the approaching man was Golconda's sheriff, Andrew Morris. He was a longtime friend of Major's parents, and after they died he'd looked after Major. Morris was the only law in town, and had been for fifteen years. As he drew his horse alongside Major's wagon, it became clear that the sheriff was worried about something. The lined face of the lawman was drawn as though pained by terrible news.

"Afternoon there, Sheriff," Major said with slow caution. He feared the revelation of whatever was eating at Morris' mind. He could not afford any delay.

"Where y'headed, Thomas?"

Major considered for a moment and replied, "Headed west. Leaving out for Indian territory."

"That don't seem right to me," said Morris. "Not at all. Why, if I was going out West, town would be about the last place I'd be headed for. In fact, Thomas, I'm sure you know that already. I guess your best bet is to get yourself turned around in the other direction."

Major was at once filled with dread. The sheriff's face was a thin disguise of civilized airs, but seething anger and disgust rippled just beneath the surface. It was something that Major had never seen before in Morris. Major took a deep breath and swallowed hard. He looked down at the ground, and the two men sat in silence until Major spoke again.

"What, exactly, is happening here?" he asked, straining to maintain a cool exterior and holster the fear that rose in his gorge.

"Preston Childers saw you walking across Burns Flats a few days ago. Said you was coming back in from the direction of the river."

The words hung in the air between them.

"That so?" Major asked in defiance of the Sheriff's strange tone.

"That's a fact," came the terse reply.

"Seems to me Preston Childers might have more pressing business besides where a grown man decides to walk in a free country." Major could feel his temper beginning to wake. It was the slow to rise, explosive-when-lit kind of temper that could set off if left to heat too long. The only actions he regretted in his life were the mistakes he'd made after giving over to his temper. The sheriff was speaking again, but not all of the words registered.

Then the trailing end of his message rang out clear: "…the filthy, lice-ridden beasts," he said. Roaming over private property, destroying farmland and stealing livestock. There's a reason we refused entry to the mangy animals. They're the walking dead, Thomas; you know that. Forsaken and cursed even by their own God."

Major tried to interrupt, but Sheriff Morris continued.

"And here you come along," he said, slinking back over the flats at first break of day, coming back from their diseased camp. What were you doing down there, Thomas? Did you go down to lie with their whore-dog women?"

The rage Major had bottled up came rushing out with all the force that had been required to keep it down. Major threw his reigns at his feet and was at the sheriff's side in one leap. He meant to beat the hate right out of the man. Major reached up to pull Morris down from the saddle when he heard the tiny click of a hammer cock back. He froze.

"Now you listen to me, son, and listen close," the sheriff hissed through his teeth. "You ain't welcome back in that town. And you ain't never gonna be again."

Major's eyes were focused dead ahead. He believed Morris had lost his mind and was set to blow out his brains.

"Hold on, Andrew. I just want to ride in, take my money out of the bank, and go. I won't stay long enough even to buy my supplies. I'll pick them up on down the trail. The next town." His anger submitted to fear now. He did not hold fear for his own death, but was terrified that his dream might die right there in the cold afternoon for no good reason at all.

"You ain't goin' back into that town for nothing." Morris said. "What kind of a man expects a decent community to expose their children to the diseases those savages carry? The sight of you makes me sick, sleeping out there among the heathens and then waltzing right back in among good Christians, carrying death right along with you. I know you've heard the reports from towns back east, and all their people cut down by disease as payment for trading with 'em."

Major's mind raced as he struggled to think with reason and not panic. "Andrew, I won't have a chance without that money. Just let me go in for what's mine, and you'll never see my face again."

"You're damn right I'll never see your face again," Morris replied with a lilt of humor in his voice, as if he had made a great joke. As Major wondered what he meant, the sheriff raised his pistol in the air and brought it down with a crack on the edge of Major's orbital bone, just at the intersection of the eye and his temple. Major's legs collapsed the moment the gun made contact. His last conscious thought was to marvel at the brilliant white sparks that burst against a lustrous red velvet curtain in the sky. Then his world went black.

The sheriff straightened himself in the saddle and holstered his revolver. He glanced down from his perch at the man lying in a heap on the ground. He looked off in the distance, in the direction the Cherokees had gone. He sucked in a long, deep breath of air through his nostrils, and a collection of mucous pooled at the back of his throat. He coughed it up held it there for a moment, tasting its salty slime. Then he expelled the green-yellow mass down on John Major's face. The cold air caused it to form a semi-solid accent on what was already a bloody slush of a mess.

"What a shame," he said aloud and kicked his spurs. The horse wheeled round and the sheriff returned to town, satisfied that his job was well done for the day.

※ ※ ※

Hundreds of miles ahead, the mood of the Cherokee refugees was shifting. While they were most decidedly still in the midst of winter, the temperatures had begun to steady consistently above freezing for several days. Bolstering their good fortune was the knowledge that Joplin, Missouri would be the last town they must pass before entering Indian Territory at long last. The land itself was important, but equally pressing was the prospect of their collective nightmare nearing its end. One in four of their brothers and sisters had been lost since the beginning of the trail ten weeks ago.

On January 13th, the Cherokee group approached the town of Joplin. Jackson Sloan led the people in a semi-circle route that skirted the outer limits of the town's borders. They did this every time they neared a town, whether it had been in Georgia or Tennessee No one wanted them close. It was best to keep out of sight and so avoid trouble. They had no reason to think that Joplin would be any different.

That winter had been the worst the South had seen in fifty years. Some people who witnessed the Cherokee whispered that the Indians carried a powerful pagan medicine that delivered them over the land. Common sense said no human beings could survive such a journey. Not even the strongest man could survive daily exposure to sub-freezing temperatures. The religious faithful crossed themselves against the evil spirits that surely travelled in the Indians' ranks. They imagined terrible worship ceremonies conducted in secret circles under the moonlight. They prayed that God would keep the pagan beasts and their dying children a safe distance from their own Christian babies.

Rachel Reese watched the road ahead with sad eyes. Rachel was happy that her people would soon find a home again, but she was torn that it would be without Major. She tried to steel herself with the acceptance that he would never come.

Her thoughts were broken by the sound of pounding hoofs close behind. She whipped around and saw two horsemen riding up. Rachel called to her father, who was walking a short distance ahead, and pointed at the two men. William halted and reached over the edge of the wagon, feeling along the side for something to defend them with, if necessary. His search turned up nothing. He turned and squared his shoulders.

But the nervous tension broke as the riders came into view and he saw they were both Cherokee brothers. These were Cherokee Baptist ministers. When they rode past the Reese wagon, one of them slowed and held up his hand in a show of respect to William. For the first time in their long three months, Rachel saw her father smile. She thought it must have been painful because his skin cracked open in the cold air, but if William was pained, he did not show it. She felt his joy at the sight of these men. She thought her father must have been the handsomest man she had ever seen, standing there covered in dried mud, his chest filled with confidence and strength once again.

The riders continued on, disappearing into the stretch of people up ahead. After half an hour or so, the line shifted back toward the south. Up ahead, they could just make out the outline of a small building with a number of people standing around. There must have been fifty tables set out with piles of items heaped up on each one. Finally, the word spread that the travellers had arrived at the Cherokee Baptist mission. The ministers had left with another Cherokee contingent a year before, and had built the mission to prepare for the thousands of their fellow tribesmen that would soon follow. They handed out blankets and shoes, corn and flagons of fresh water. All of the people in Sloan's contingent set up camp in a broad circle that surrounded the mission church.

Hot bowls of broth were passed around, along with enough corn cakes to feed every mouth present. For the first time in two and a half months, not a single mouth went without food that night. At last the people would have a full night's rest, with warm bodies and full stomachs. But before any of them would lie down and rest, all two hundred sixty-seven of them gathered together and offered up the gift of their voices to the heavens, praising Yowa for their deliverance into the trusted hands of their brethren, and for accepting the souls of the ones that were left behind on the trail.

Their worship was sublime in its gratitude, as it had been every Sunday since leaving Georgia. No matter where they found themselves out in the vast expanse of the wilderness, despite the freezing temperatures outside and regardless of a desperate need to press on, the group spent every single Sunday, without exception, gathered together to offer praise to their omniscient Creator.

The next morning saw the people rise up from the ground like the first tender shoots of spring. The Cherokee sensed the end to their long trail was nigh. Within two days they would cross into Indian Territory at its northeastern-most point. From there, the ministers said, they would continue for another three days to the south, to the new Cherokee capitol. It was rumored to nestle in a fertile river valley in a thick wilderness filled with game and streams stocked with fish.

Rachel was delighted to find that, overnight, she was able to imagine her old home again. The vision of it appeared to her in a dream, and when she awoke she felt that it was a message, ensuring that the people would find another life ahead; a fruitful, blessed one in which their children would have the resources to thrive and maintain their noble, ancient culture.

Though she clung to this vision, she could not surrender fully to its grandeur. Part of her felt trapped on the icy riverbank, still waiting for Major. She pictured him back in Golconda, on his homestead working the fields. Her heart was sorrowful for his broken promise.

His absence compounded the disappointment Rachel felt when they passed from Missouri into Indian Territory. The land here was not as they had described at all. When the family set up for camp, they found that the soil here was impossibly stony and tinged with metal, the most unusual land they had come across. William assured them that the land would become green and fertile as they journeyed closer to their new home.

Some of the people spoke in hushed voices of a strange glowing light that had been spotted following the travelers from a distance. A few of the men had broken away to try and chase down the light to discover its source, but they returned without their quarry and with no explanation for its origin. Other small groups were terrified by it, convinced it was a harbinger of death. They carried on through the night in order to put distance between themselves and a land that bore such ominous things.

William reminded his family that they were in no danger because the people were under protection of a greater power. He explained that the light might be a barn owl. They sometimes lined their nests with a phosphorescent moss that settled onto their feathers when they nested, giving them a greenish, ghostly glow when they took to the air. Rachel and Ani nodded at his explanation and were pleased to think the thing might be explained away by an incredible act of nature.

None of them were bothered by the sight of the light that first evening, and the next day they rose to pack their things for one of the last times. Ani dumped the leftover water into the fire, and steam flew up and sent a lengthy hiss into the air. She looked up through the fog and gasped.

There, at the edge of their camp, stood a bizarre, unsteady figure just at the boundary of the tree line. She cried out for William, who was looking after the animals. He came running, but Rachel had gotten to her feet. The ragged, emaciated figure was Thomas Major who, at long last, had arrived to fulfill his promise. Rachel ran to his side and helped him to a seat beside the dampened fire.

Ani came to bring him water. He was shaking and so overcome by weakness that he could not bring the water to his own mouth without help. Rachel knelt before him and stared up at his skeletal visage. He must have lost thirty pounds in the course of just two weeks. Half of his handsome dark brow was gone, and in its place was a deep wound that looked at least a week old; a thick brown scab had grown over the top of it.

"Thomas, what happened to you?" Rachel asked in a small voice.

His dejected gaze lifted at the sound of her voice, and the sight of her burned off part of the fog that surrounded his mind. He felt his strength could be regained if he just stayed close to her. After he took another sip of water, he began to tell them the story of his flight to find his way back to Rachel.

He had awakened in unspeakable pain on the ground, his blood and a flap of his own scalp dried against his face. The pain burned like a malevolent entity holding him hostage in his own body. After lying awake for what seemed like hours, he was able to drag himself up into the wagon. His horses remained nearby, and they were the only reason for his survival.

He told them, without going into too much detail, that he was not able to retrieve his savings from the bank and had only the provisions from home to sustain him for the duration of the journey. He passed by the home of a kind family who put him up for a night and gave him the little extra stores of corn and fat from their pantry. They implored that he wait until the local doctor could come and tend to his battered head, but he politely refused and left before daybreak the next morning, still in pursuit. After his team made it across the thawing Mississippi, the wagon's wheels became hopelessly buried in over a foot of thick, cold river mud. By then the horses were starving and had not eaten for five days. He unbridled them and beat them until they ran from him into the forest. He knew it was the only chance they might have to survive.

After Major finished his story, William remained silent for some time. His mind stewed with a question, the answer to which he feared in his heart. Everyone waited in silence, because they could see that William was troubled. At last, he leaned back and crossed his arms over his chest. His voice was measured and controlled, as if by great discipline on his part.

"Thomas Major, our family owes you a debt we can never repay for the gifts of medicine and food you brought to us that night on the plain. Your kindness will never be forgotten." He paused and then went on, "But you must tell me, because I do not understand. Why have you left your home at such peril to follow the Cherokee to this place?"

Major's mouth fell open as though he were a fish left to die on a creek bank. In all the miles between this place and his home, during all the imaginary conversations he'd hoped might happen with Rachel's family, this one was not a possibility. He'd been sure that, by now, Rachel would have declared their plans to her parents; that she would have already told them of his impending arrival. He looked at her for an answer and saw shame in her eyes that confirmed she had kept their plans a secret.

But hadn't William and Ani noticed the two of them speaking so intimately the night he followed her down to the Cherokee camp? They must have recognized the obvious sight of two people falling in love. But for all the excuses Major ran through in his head, he knew that William waited for an answer, and that he must speak up. He realized that the words he spoke might be the most important of his entire life.

"William," he said, "you and I are friends. We come from different worlds, but as men we are similar. Our existence is made from the land with hard work. Your family, after your devotion to the Creator, is your priority and the ambition of your life. You do not serve greed; you serve love. This is the way I see my life: a life like yours, with your daughter by my side.

"I left everything that represented my old life behind. To find Rachel, I left it buried in the mud. I ask you now not to deny me this new life. I am here to ask your permission, and the permission of your wife, to marry Rachel. You ask me why I made this journey, but even as I speak I can see that you already knew the answer to your own question."

For much of his speech, Major held William's gaze to make his sincerity plain. But as the last of his words were spoken, his eyes looked to Rachel and saw that she was smiling. Ani was the most difficult to read because she sat motionless, with her head down. Her hands sat in her lap, fidgeting with the hem of her apron. Major thought her reservation curious. He would later realize that her muted behavior was in anticipation of William's response, which she could have predicted beforehand with unwavering certainty.

Agitated, William rose to a standing position. "You do not belong with us."

Major stood with him. He winced as a stab of pain cut through his battered temple like a hot blade.

"You should return to your own people," said William. "We are not the same, as you say. My daughter will marry a son of the Cherokee; this is meant to be. We will not accept a white soldier, one from among many who drove our people from our own lands at the end of a bayonet point. One from among those whose hands have been stained red by the blood of our people, who dropped onto the frozen land like fallen trees, one after the next. Their blood will never be washed away from this land."

The air was thick with emotion, and William paused to restrain himself. The image of his mother's body in the cold cave passed before his vision.

Before he could begin again, a panicked and desperate Rachel spoke up. Her voice sounded shrill and childlike. The words spoken by William filled her with righteous anger. She knew that her father's words came from a bitter place that had grown in his heart. A black, rotten, acrid place that grew stronger with each passing day on the trail, as he watched loved ones die around him. This was his protective response to the fear that he would not manage to keep his family alive until they reached their new home. It was the fear that had grown in him to cause this bitterness.

Rachel knew that neither truth nor justice could be born out of fear. She also knew that her father would not be moved on a subject once he had spoken on it, but she felt that her own words represented their only chance to show him that he was wrong this time.

"I do love him. You know this well, because you have seen it with your own eyes. Your eyes have also shown you that this is a soldier who removed us from our home." Her words fell unrestrained from her mouth, as a swollen stream from the side of a mountain. "Look at him, Father. This is the one who saved the life of Mahala. I was the one who summoned him from his sleep, a stranger on his doorstep in the darkest hour of the night. He would have been within all reason to have shot me where I stood, beating upon his door and demanding his presence in a camp of sick people, who, as far as he knew, were just as likely to kill him as greet him."

"He has never known our people before now. How is it that he found the courage to gather his own medicine and travel in the dark to give it away to a people unknown to him? I cannot explain this. And neither can you. Can you say you would have done the same? Would you have given your own medicine to save the life a strange group of travelers passing through? Truly, Father, I cannot say you would!"

William remained silent and allowed Rachel to speak. She had never spoken to him in this way. He knew she cared for the man.

Rachel continued, "Look at his hands. These are not the hands that carried the bayonets. They are the hands that brought healing to Mahala. It was the river ice that took her from us." Rachel's cheeks had become flushed as she suddenly became self-aware. She had been speaking as though the words were not her own, but instead a body of water that flowed through her like a vessel. Like water from a pitcher to a glass. Now she found that her nervousness had returned, and the ease with which she found her voice vanished. Her hands, which were animated by her fiery plea, dropped useless to her sides. She felt more helpless than ever in her life, and with the last of her resolve repeated the words she'd begun with: "I do love him."

William collected himself in the wake of her powerful will.

"You are still young, Rachel," he said. "Your feelings are strong like your words, and I know that truth is carried in them."

Rachel, whose head had dropped as William spoke, looked up in surprise at his admission. Perhaps this was a sign that his mind was changed.

"Major." He turned to address Thomas. "Please forgive me. I spoke out of anger. You deserve my deepest respect.

"We will not send you back alone into the wilderness after you have done these things for our family and sacrificed so much. You will travel with us to the capital. It is only a two-day journey from here. We will leave in the morning after you have had a night to rest. Ani will care for your head, and Rachel will make your dinner."

He had not yet spoken on the only subject that mattered most, and Major felt that his brain might explode from his head if

William did not finish. At last, William spoke his final words on the subject of Thomas and Rachel.

"Rachel, your heart is tender. You have been changed by the things you have witnessed. It is not time yet for you to find a husband. But when it is time, and your mind has been healed from the loss of your home and your people, you will find that you wish to make a family with a Cherokee man. When we reach the capital, Thomas Major will leave and make his own way. This is my decision, and we will not speak of it again."

William turned and walked from the camp to signal the end of the discussion. Rachel's head fell into her hands, and her lean frame was rocked by bitter sobs. Ani stood at her daughter's side and watched helplessly, for the time had come when Rachel did not need the solace of her mother.

Rachel left her mother's side and fell into the arms of Major. His arms, that had once been solid like the branches of an oak, were now weak and frail. The realization that Major endured so much for her was more than she could bear. The future she saw in her dreams with vibrant enthusiasm began to slip away. She held tight to Major because she felt certain the grief would swallow her whole.

Major stood stoic and did not betray any emotion. Ani turned away and walked out of sight to allow them a measure of privacy in their sorrow.

When Ani was gone, Major slipped his hand into Rachel's hair, his fingers gently touching her ear. He dropped his head low, so that his mouth was at the side of her head. Her wretched sobs were subsiding now, but her chest continued to hitch violently. From a distance the pair appeared to be wrapped in a loving embrace. But appearances are often deceiving, and such was their grip on one another.

"Tonight," Major said. "Come to the ridge overlooking the river. I will wait for you."

With that he withdrew his hand and slid his fingertips over her soft cheek as he went. He strode away in the direction from which he had come. Rachel stood and watched him go, reeling at the gravity unfolding before her.

Her eyes remained full of tears, waiting for just one more drop in order to spill over the edge and join the rest. She stood in disbelief, realizing that whole chapters of her life had been written or erased, and that all of this had happened without her own consent.

William returned to camp and saw Rachel standing alone, her dark eyes full of water as they watched the east. There was no need to inquire about the absence of Thomas Major. He'd known that Major would leave, and this was the proper order of life. Once they reached the new land and were reunited with the rest of the Cherokee, Rachel would find her old friends and fall in love with one of them. Someday, when she had children of her own, she would realize her foolishness and blush at this memory. Rachel's father shook his head at her youthful lack of foresight and walked back to the wagon. As he approached the edge of camp, a keen sense of dread entered his heart and stopped him cold in his tracks. But he steeled himself and, by sheer stubborn will, forced the spirit to pass away. William interpreted the unfamiliar sense as a weak empathy for Rachel's tears, rather than the harbinger of danger for which it was intended.

Chapter 9

Shell

> *Oh mother, tell your children not to do what I have done.*
> The Animals, "House of the Rising Sun"

Leonard woke up in an excited state the next morning. The windows in the bedroom were covered with heavy drapes, and the room was silent, dark, and cool. He had no way of guessing the time. But he felt renewed and certain it must already be daylight out.

Shell was lying in the bed with her back to him. Her body temperature ran hot. She put off enough heat to raise the temperature of the entire room. Len rested his hand a few inches away from her just to be close to that warmth. He forced himself to resist the urge to move closer and hold on to her. She hadn't come to bed until very late the night before. He knew she would want to sleep in before they continued on their road trip later that day.

Len lay on his back and looked up again, this time into the darkness of the room.

I can make things different today, he told himself, *I can show her she can't make it, that she doesn't want to live without me. She's going to change her mind and realize how good we are together. Really good together.*

The thought of forming a plan, of exerting some control over the situation, filled Len with a restored energy; now was the time to get started. He carefully lifted up the edge of the comforter and slid his feet and legs out of the bed until they touched the floor. Shell had laid both their robes out on the bedside chair, and it was a good thing because otherwise he would have to turn on the light. Feeling his way across the wall in the dark, he reached the chair and grabbed the robes. He reached across the darkness, shuffling his socked feet on the floor until he blindly bumped an outstretched finger against the door handle. He hurriedly opened the door and stepped out into the dim hallway, shutting the door behind him. He wanted to let Shell sleep in as long as possible. They had big plans for the day ahead, and he wanted her to be rested and ready for the things to come.

Once outside the bedroom, Leonard looked down and realized he had an erection. There he was in the middle of the Foster family hall, pitching a tent—and a rather respectable one at that. God forbid some family member happened by and saw *that* thing flying full mast. He stood still in the hallway for a second and hoped he was the only one awake. Then he heard the low growl of coffee percolating in the kitchen. Someone was already up and stirring. He took a quick stride across the hallway and into the bathroom. He could stay in there and clean up, at least until Little Leonard Jr. calmed down and took a break from sentry duty.

Len stepped up to the mirror above the sink, stroking his chin and giving himself a long, honest look in the mirror. He frowned at his reflection, not because he was dissatisfied with the image, but because the strange contortion of his face amused him. "Not bad," he said out loud. He turned his face to one side and then the other, eyes remaining fixed on the reflection ahead. He tilted his chin up and stroked his neck. It already felt rough and covered with stubble. No surprise there; he needed to shave again. He looked down to note that his pelvic area was still in an extreme state of petrifaction.

Should have stayed in bed, he thought to himself. Shell could have relieved this uncomfortable state he was in. Sometimes if he touched her while she was still deep asleep she woke up aroused and aggressive. He thought of her voice, gravelly and sensuous when she first awakened in the morning. He wondered if he should try to slip back across the hall and back into bed. As he considered this, he slipped a hand down into the front of his boxers and grabbed hold of himself. He looked back up into the mirror and recognized the intense and rather desperate look of sexual desire in his own eyes. He pulled his hand back out of his shorts and turned on the cold water spigot. The water pooled in his cupped hands and he splashed it onto his face.

No, of course she won't be in the mood right now, he told himself. *Not here.* All the feelings of jealousy came flooding back from the night before. If he could have wished the Foster family from the earth, save Shell, he would have done so in that very instant.

He forced himself into a state of calm because he knew that if he lost his temper again in front of her family it would amount to the "be all end all" and a coup de grace as the paramour of Shell Foster. Leonard ran his hand down from the brow to the mouth and thought for a moment. *Maybe later tonight when we're outside. Just the two of us on a blanket in the dark.*

Len decided that his best approach would be to satiate himself with thoughts of their evening plans and forget the idea of going back to the bedroom. He moved over to the toilet, lifted the lid, and stood staring straight down at his penis, which had begun to flag at long last. He had begun to fear it might hold him hostage here in the bathroom for the duration of the morning. "Like a Russian racehorse," he thought to himself, well-pleased as he finally accomplished a good, long morning piss. The rushing stream of urine hit the water and foamed up. He flushed the toilet a few seconds before he was finished, watching gravity pull the golden urine funnel into the ground.

Shell's robe was lying on the floor below his, which was still hanging from a wall hook. *I must have accidentally grabbed them both,* he thought. He wrapped his own robe around his body, picked Shell's off the floor, and hung it up. He washed his hands and walked out toward the kitchen.

Len casually sauntered past the kitchen entryway, his mind still lingering on the evening to come, when he stopped in his tracks. He could hardly trust his own eyes, but there was Shell in her robe at the stove, already up and fiddling around with a couple of pans. She must not have heard him shuffle down the hall in his socks because her back was turned to him and she hadn't noticed his presence behind her. A rubber band held her dark hair in a knot at the back of her neck.

Strange, he thought, *why did she bring two robes along?* He shrugged off his hesitation.

Len tip-toed across the kitchen floor and shot his arms out around the waist in front of him and pulled her backward against his body.

"*Aiiee!*" She let out a startled screech. She turned to face Len and he was struck at once by the horrifying realization that this was not Shell up making breakfast in the kitchen, but Shell's mother, Christie.

"Holy *SHIT*, Mrs. Foster; I'm sorry, I thought you were Shell, I swear to God I did!"

Christie Foster had already begun to compose herself after the initial shock, though her hands were grasping the front lapels of her robe as if they might fly open of their own accord. She began to laugh, but still she raised a hand to the side of her face, which had turned a deep crimson. Leonard felt the blood rising to spread over his own face too. This came as a great surprise to him. He could count the number of times he had blushed in his life on one hand.

"Leonard Harris, that's some way to greet an old lady in the morning!" she joked, in an attempt to set him at ease. She was a master at that; people always felt comfortable around Christie. She could hardly go to the local grocery store without some poor soul offering up his life story.

The two laughed together while avoiding eye contact. She handed him a coffee cup. "I think you better get yourself some caffeine and quick, Son, to clear your head," she said, nodding in the direction of the coffee maker.

"In that robe, from behind, you…" His voice trailed off. He was still blushing. "You know, you look a lot like Shell."

"You're not the first person to confuse the two of us," she said in an effort to reassure him. "I always take it as a compliment, to tell the truth. I promise I won't breathe a word of this to anyone else as long as you don't either. They'll all make fun of us for the rest of the morning if they get word—especially Jennifer."

"You don't have to worry about me," Len snorted, relieved by the chance to change the subject. "Listen, I want to apologize for my behavior last night, Mrs. Foster. I don't have any good excuse other than being worn out from the drive, and, to be honest, Shell and I hadn't been getting along too well. But I shouldn't have acted like that…I just had a 'moment,' that's all. I hope you and Dean can forgive me for it."

"You've already been forgiven, Leonard," Christie said. "We knew you were tired. Dean was worried about you two last night. He hardly slept a lick. He'll be glad to know you aren't angry still. Not that it's any of my business, and you don't have to say if you don't want to, but what *is* the trouble between you and Shell?"

Len sat down on a barstool at the white oak island and thought for a moment. He considered whether he should discuss his problems with Shell with her mother. He knew Shell would object to such an intimate conversation. She vehemently objected to any public mention of information beyond casual details. She was his mirror opposite in this regard, since he'd always believed that an open, honest discussion was always the most rational way to solve any problem.

But his concern that Shell might object was overridden by an irresistible desire to purge his insecurity about the relationship, so he began to tell everything. He told Christie that Shell had grown distant over the past several months, and that he didn't know why or how to fix it; He told her how much he loved Shell—more than she knew—and that he couldn't—wouldn't, actually—imagine his life without her.

Christie Foster let Leonard do most of the talking while she moved around the kitchen making breakfast. The house was quiet except for the sound of bacon sizzling on the stove and the tireless voice of Leonard Harris.

"One thing that bothers me most about Shell is that I've never seen her cry," he said. No matter how bad the fight gets—and they've been really bad at times; I admit I've said some nasty things to her. I mean, only because she'd said some pretty nasty things first, and I wanted to make her feel as terrible as she made me feel. But no matter what happens, she never cries. Not a single drop. My entire life I've never met a girl who couldn't cry. Makes me think she doesn't care one way or the other."

"Oh no, Len; you shouldn't think that way. I'll tell you something funny about Shell." Christie Foster leaned her hip against the edge of the counter, stirring pancake mix as she spoke. "She didn't even cry when she was born. Came out cool as a cucumber; looked around the room and up at us like there was no surprise at all. Like she already knew what to expect. Seems strange, I know, especially for a girl, but Shell just doesn't cry. Never has. Then, of course, being the oldest child and watching out for Jennifer all these years—well, I guess it made her that much more resilient. You shouldn't read anything personal into that. Crying just isn't part of her nature, that's all."

Len was filled with such relief at this simple explanation. His furrowed brow relaxed and he leaned back in his chair a bit.

Christie used a fork to flip a pancake out of the pan and onto a plate. She sat the plate down on the island in front of Len with some softened butter, maple syrup, and peanut butter. He sat in a daydream, staring down at the food with a distracted smile plastered across his face.

"Orange juice or chocolate milk?" she asked him. "Or will you take more coffee?"

He snapped back to attention and looked at Christie with a smile. "Just more coffee, Mrs. Foster. Thank you."

"Ah, Len, you've been coming here with Shell for what, going on three years now? Call us by our first names. You might have noticed we aren't too formal about things in this house."

"Ok, Christie, I think I will," he said with a smirk, and shoveled a forkful of pancake and peanut butter into his mouth. The door at the end of the hall opened and Dean Foster scooted down the hall toward the kitchen. He poured himself a cup of coffee and wordlessly sat down across from Len. Any trace of anger from the evening before had been erased from his face by six or so hours of repose. Christie made a plate with pancakes and bacon for herself, and one for her husband. She sat down to share breakfast, and the three of them spent the next hour deep in conversation while the two girls slept.

By the time Shell got up and showered, the sun was already high and bright overhead. Lunch was on the table: soup and sandwiches. Len reclined in a chair with his book. He looked up from his reading when she walked in.

"Look at you, all shiny and clean," he said, holding out his hand. She was surprised at his countenance. His eyes sparkled—he seemed ecstatic. It was a shocking change from the night before, and rather unexpected.

She smiled wanly and reached out to meet his grasp. "Thanks, I feel so much better. Can you believe it's already noon? I haven't slept this late in years."

"That must have been some conversation you and your sister had last night," he said, looking up at her.

She pulled her hand away, cocked her head sideways, and began to brush the tangles from her wet hair.

"No, not really; not a whole lot of talking at all." The words fell from her mouth in rapid-fire succession and her voice rose as she spoke the lie. "It's always the same thing every time. We just stare up at nothingness. Hey, why do you have that funny look on your face?" she asked. She was nervous and thought that he might have overheard her conversation with Jenny. *But that isn't possible*, she told herself.

"Nothing," he said. "I'm just excited to get to Hornetsville…Or whatever the name of the place is."

She raised an eyebrow, wondering what could have possibly made Leonard enthusiastic about the Spooklight.

"Have I got a surprise for *you*," he said.

"I'm not sure how to feel about that," she said, and her crooked grin turned down. She loved surprises, but there was something in the curious way he delivered the line that gave her pause. "No surprises, Len. It's just a long drive up to a little place in the woods to try and see a ghost. We aren't even supposed to speak while we're watching for the light. So no surprises. I'm serious." She hesitated, and then added, "unless, of course, the light is real. Then we'll have the biggest surprise of our lives. If you try to scare me, I'll never speak to you again."

Len dropped his book into his lap and dog-eared the page. He addressed her in a mysterious tone that she did not quite recognize. He was hiding something.

"Lighten up," he said, sounding for all the world like he was hiding something. "I'm not going to try to scare you. This is going to be fun, babe."

He grabbed her around the hips and pulled her to him. She plopped rather awkwardly onto his lap, not expecting the sudden force. He grunted a bit as she landed. Shell's father walked into the room just as she sat down. She felt embarrassed to be seen on Len's lap, like some kind of stupid teenager. She smiled at her father across the room.

"I was thinking about this all night," her father began, "and if you two insist on going up there to look for the Spooklight, I have a couple of requirements you'll have to agree to."

Here we go again. Preach it Brothuh Fostuh, she mused, imagining the words in the style of televangelist Jimmy Swaggart's voice.

"I want you to drive my pickup truck."

This instruction was not what she'd expected, and Shell sat up quickly to protest.

"Dad, we can't drive your truck; we're not coming back through this way. We're going to hop on 412 and drive back to the city," she said. She could imagine little worse than being forced to drive back to her parents' home late that night, then wake up and drive all the way back home on Sunday. They would be exhausted.

"I have to be back at work first thing Monday morning, so we just really can't come back through this way."

"That's fine if you don't want to come back here tonight," her father replied. "Just take my truck and keep it. We'll swap back the next time you come home to visit."

Shell looked at him, still not convinced.

"Look," he continued, "you're going to be driving down a bunch of rough, old country roads once you get up there. I can't say for sure, because I've never been to Spooklight Road, but you may even have to drive over a couple of low water bridges. There's no telling what could happen if you drove that little car up there. You'll get stuck. Or have a flat. Just do it for me," he said, no longer asking, but rather commanding Shell. "Then I won't have to worry about you getting stranded out in B.F.E."

"I guess I can drive your truck," she said. But I hope you realize I may not be able to bring it back here until Thanksgiving." She hoped that would change his mind. He would need his truck before then; Thanksgiving was three weeks away.

But her father did not hesitate. "That's okay. Just go ahead and take it. Hell, if something comes up and I need a truck I'll just borrow your Grandpa's."

Shell had no more points to offer in response, so at last gave up her protest.

Len picked up the conversation. "What about navigation?" he asked. "We don't know exactly how to get to this place, do we?"

"Just go back toward Tahlequah," said Dean. "Turn north on Highway 10. Take it all the way past Grove, and then head east on old 19. Eventually you have to turn off the pavement and drive the final miles on dirt. I imagine you'll have to stop and ask directions from a local once you get up there. When you get way back on those old dirt roads, you'll find that no electronics work. No GPS, not even your cell phones."

"Let's just take Dad's state map and do it the old fashioned way," Shell said, grabbing Len's wrist and giving it a little squeeze. She put her hands on both sides of the recliner and pushed herself up and onto her feet. "Come on, we'd better get started and load up the truck."

She walked back to the guest room and began to hurriedly pack their clothes and shoes. Undergarments and socks had been strewn about the room in the dark. With the light turned on and the window drapes pushed back, Shell haphazardly dashed the lot of it into their bags.

When she finished packing her suitcase, she pulled out its handle and stood it upright, then slung the strap of Len's black duffel bag across her chest. *There,* she thought, *now we're ready to go.* She propped the door open with her backside and pulled the suitcase out into the hall. She would have died before she asked for any help from Len after the Oscar performance from the night before. But he was already walking toward her from the living room and took the heaviest bag with a sheepish smile. He hadn't apologized for the outburst, but at least she saw in his face that if he could wish it away, he would.

They walked into the living room together, each of them carrying a bag. There sat Shell's family, all three of them together on the couch, each of their faces awash in a sober countenance.

"You three look like you're seeing us off to the firing squad," Shell joked.

"We just wish you could stay longer," her mother said.

"You just got here," said Jenny. "Why don't you just stay one more night? I have a bad feeling. Just don't go."

"Can't," said Shell with a wink. "We've got people to do and things to see." "I'll call you as soon as we get back home." She exchanged a knowing glance with her sister and walked on.

Dean Foster held the heavy front door open for Len and Shell. They carried their bags out, and Len hoisted them into the bed of the pickup truck. He was annoyed by the disorganized clutter of tools, gas cans, and errant scraps of metal piled in the back.

At the driver's side, Dean handed Shell his keys. A Bob Dylan key ring hung off of them with the symbol of the all-seeing eye. "Remember what I said," he reminded her.

"Okay, Dad, I will." She reached her arms up around his shoulders and gave him a big hug. Then she walked over to her mother and sister who stood waiting on the front porch.

"I love you," she said, and kissed each of them once on the cheek.

Soon they would all remember that last farewell and weep with regret that they had not made it last longer.

Chapter 10

Shell

> *I'm a thousand miles from nowhere,*
> *time don't matter to me.*
> Dwight Yoakum,
> "A Thousand Miles from Nowhere"

"Seriously, Len; I don't think Spooklight Road is the kind of place for surprises," Shell repeated again. She could not shake the eerie vibe she felt, and for her life had no idea what he might be hiding. "You're supposed to be quiet and still when you get there. No talking or anything like that, if you want to see the light."

"Great, no talking, I'm on board with that." Len reached over and started the music again. His brow was knitted, so she knew he was mulling something over in his mind. Preoccupied. Shell preferred when he spoke without ceasing. The quiet Len was a strange and unfamiliar one, and his contemplative state filled her with a strong sense of unease.

Life's the same, I'm moving in stereo; life's the same, except for my shoes, Ric Ocasek moaned from the speakers. From the sound of his voice and the music, his trepidation matched her own—though she thought Len's selections so far made the perfect road tripping music, all buzzed and spacey. Eventually the music helped change the mood and made Shell giddy with anticipation. She imagined herself standing out in a dark alfalfa field surrounded by beautiful little lights floating all around.

She was glad they had set out with plenty of daylight left. They crossed the river bridge again, this time traveling west. Len flashed the signal to turn right onto Highway 10. The view along this drive was beautiful in its stark autumn frieze. On the left, great solemn cliffs hung out over the road. To the right, the cold and dark Illinois River snaked alongside them. The elegant limbs of the blackjack oaks reached overhead and stretched to rendezvous with the cliffs midway over the road, braiding together in a maleficent archway. The road stretched out before them in a dark, shiftless charcoal line scribbled out upon the earth, marking out the pathway to an object that existed in Shell's mind only in the most abstract fashion. She hoped that, after tonight, this would no longer be the case. She wanted to see the Spooklight like the Cars said, *moving in stereo.*

Shell was in the driver's seat this time. Len had offered, but she thought it would be best she for her to drive since the pickup belonged to her father. Len didn't mind all that much, since he had a few things to mull over. After breakfast that morning, Len had been struck by the realization that he had to ask Shell to marry him while they were out on the road. He knew she was slipping away, and though he did not understand the reasons why, he realized now that reasons did not matter. What mattered was keeping her; he would not just throw up his hands and allow Shell to walk away. So at breakfast that morning, in full acceptance of this new-found epiphany, he asked Dean and Christie Foster for permission to marry their daughter.

Their reaction had not been at all what he might have hoped. They were both taken aback in the beginning, and they were not sly enough to disguise it. That was the thing with most people. If you surprised a person, there was a fraction of a second during which you could read the absolute truth written on their face. Give a person even the slightest bit of warning, and they could be emotionally prepared with a poker face, or even worse a false reaction. If a man was keen enough, he could read anybody; see all their innermost truths in just a matter of seconds. Leonard might have expected a less-than-ebullient reaction on the part of the Fosters anyway—his behavior the night before had rather guaranteed that. He accepted their hesitancy and then set about to change their minds.

Len was a man who, above all other things, had great confidence in his own intellect. He did not consider himself better than most other people, but he did consider himself cleverer. He had no doubt that with just the right amount of flattery and cajoling he could get the Fosters to accept that their daughter could be happy with him. Not that their permission mattered all that much to him. But he knew Shell would be charmed to know that he'd asked their permission. She was old fashioned in a few strange ways. He didn't consider Jenny. Her disdain for him bubbled just below the surface, and he returned the sentiment. He knew that it was a struggle for her to tolerate his presence, and she never made much effort to disguise it. *Oh, she is a hard-headed, difficult twit,* he thought. His solution was to dismiss her from consideration. She was not an integer in the formula. She was Shell's baby sister. How much sway could she really have in the matter? Not enough to be concerned with, he reckoned.

As they rode along this time, it was Leonard who recognized an old favorite song on the playlist. A couple of decades had come and gone since he'd listened to Springsteen's *Born in the U.S.A.*, but when it first came out in the 1980s he was a man obsessed. The shortest track was his favorite. He only remembered the chorus, but emerged from his embroiled thoughts long enough to sing that: *only you can cool my desire; ooo, ooo, hoo, I'm on fire.*

He thought Shell would be amused that he knew the words and stole a glance toward the driver's seat, but her eyes were locked dead ahead in whatever strange, orb-filled world she had floating around her mind. For once, he did not feel the need to capture her attention. He was glad to have her distracted so he could really think out the evening's events. His mind darted off and returned to his breakfast conversation with her parents.

※ ※ ※

They'd been engaged in small talk for the entirety of the first fifteen minutes, and Leonard's conscious mind barely registered any of the topics Christie brought up. He contributed a nod of agreement and a bemused smile from time to time, but all along his thoughts were stuck on making a proposal that night. His mind was made up. He scooted the orange-yellow scrambled egg curd to the edge of his scalloped plate and waited for a chance to change the subject.

His hearing tuned back in to their conversation. "I agree; the way they fixed up that old place is just incredible! I wonder where they found that moonflower plant," Shell's mother was saying.

"Mmhmm. Looks like a lot of work though," Dean had replied, ignoring the moonflower question altogether.

It was just the kind of conversation that would have pissed Shell off. He, at least, knew that much about her, while her parents did not. He realized that there were a number of ways in which he knew her better, and that made him feel most satisfied. He knew she loved her family unconditionally, but there were some things she didn't trust with them and never spoke of in their presence. There were some things that they didn't know, but that he did.

He cleared his throat to interrupt. "Erm, Mr. and Mrs. Foster, pardon my interruption, and I hope I'm not overstepping my bounds here, but…"

He was stopped mid-sentence by Shell's father: "It's Dean and Christie, Leonard. Please, relax around us."

"I told him the very same thing not thirty minutes ago," Christie added with a singsong cheerfulness that annoyed Len. Where he came from, the thought of ever referring to a friend's parents by their first names meant poor, common manners. And while most people would find the Fosters' folksy charm endearing, he felt certain they overplayed the part, and he was forced to grit his teeth at the sound of their strong country accents. Until he'd heard them speak, he'd never realized that Shell carried the well-disguised remnants of a rural accent she must have tamed years ago.

Must have taken her years of practice to rid herself of the thick, awkward twang, he thought. *And thank God she did.* He was certain that if her voice had rung that country bell on the day their fated paths crossed, he would have turned right around and walked away.

After agreeing to Mr. Foster's insistence at informality, Len began in a very measured, subtle way to clear the field in order to march his plan through. He asked the Fosters the details of how they first met. High school sweetheart, of course, *how perfectly typical*, Leonard thought to himself.

Christie Foster was thrilled to have the subject introduced and went through what must have been every possible detail of the courtship from the first glimpse to the wedding. Her prose on the topic carried on at exhaustive length; at least ten minutes. She was the first one on the hook. People loved to talk about themselves; he knew that very well from personal experience.

Now on to Dean, he thought. Shell's father would be the most difficult one to convince, at least by his own estimation. Second only to Jenny, of course, but then, she was not to be considered.

"Right, Christie, so you fell head over heels for the high school football star?"

She laughed at that, and when her eyes met Dean's over the table, Leonard noticed that even after so many years mutual admiration remained between the two. He could not detect any passion at all, but at least they hadn't gone through some tacky mid-life crisis divorce like so many others their age. The idea of middle-aged daters was repugnant to him, and he knew that once he and Shell were married it would be the end of his worries over her. She would not be the type to leave her husband; she had at least learned that much from her own parents.

His attention turned back to Dean. Though nearly fifty, Shell's father still sat at attention at the mention of football.

"What position did you play, Dean?" Len asked. Touchdown. That one subject was all the effort required to win him over.

Leonard sat back and marveled at his own social skill. This was his first real attempt at charming either one of the elder Fosters. He had always conducted himself properly in their company, he felt, and minded proper manners in past visits, but had never gone to the trouble of winning them over. He quite liked the feeling of having both their attention and appreciation.

Len felt sure the moment to introduce his idea to them had arrived. He had to wait with great patience as Dean Foster described, at length, the excruciating moment on the gridiron, where he acquired his dreaded shoulder injury from an illegal hit that required immediate surgery and ultimately spelled the end of his football career. Len lowered his head in reverence at the end of Dean's story and shook it from side to side to demonstrate his disgust at the awful hand that fate dealt to Dean Foster and his shoulder. A shared sense of manly sorrow and camaraderie was born between them. He gave Dean a quick pat on the back, but that gesture seemed to have gone just a bit too far, as both registered an awkward pause.

"Look," Len said. It was his favorite word to begin a persuasive argument. *Look*. Most politicians used the word when answering a question on the Sunday morning news programs. It had at some point become the word *du jour* for demanding attention and declaring the veracity of the unbelievable string of absurdity to follow.

"Look," he had said, and the Fosters leaned forward, reeled in by the command of the word, "I came here with Shell for a reason. And not for the same reason she came."

The color of breakfast conversation made a sudden turn from the sentimental to the weighty. He could see the curiosity in Christie Foster's eyes.

"What do you mean?" she half-whispered in a cartoonish, breathy voice.

"You didn't really believe I came all the way down here to chase after a phantom light, did you? I would hope you held me in higher regard." He paused to allow them the opportunity to agree, that yes, they did hold him in higher regard.

"From the moment Shell brought this ridiculous story up," he continued, "she was hysterical about going to hunt the thing down. She didn't even recall it on her own. She had been watching some reruns of an old show. *Unsolved Mysteries* or something like that."

"That was one of her favorite shows when she was a little girl," said Dean.

Len carried on as if he hadn't heard. "She was curled up in her chair watching this show, and they did a segment about the Hornet Spooklight, and she jumped up in her chair like she was stuck by lightning. She started shouting for me to watch, to pay attention, and asked if I'd heard of it before, and of course I had not; then she was shouting for me to shut up and watch. I thought maybe she had downed one too many glasses of wine… She's been doing more and more of that just lately." He threw that part in so that they would consider him the responsible one in the relationship. Plus, she *had* been drinking much more than usual these days, so it wasn't a complete lie. "But when she woke up the next morning, her mind was made up. She was going to go try and see that damned ghost light. Or will-o'-the-wisp. Whatever."

Shell's parents nodded in agreement, though they could not anticipate Len's point. He was bobbing and weaving, putting on a show—trying to throw them off center so their minds would really be blown at the grand conclusion.

"The real reason I came with Shell this weekend was to have the chance to talk to you two."

From his vantage point at the table, Len could not see Dean's full expression, but he reveled in the slow realization that was unfolding across Christie's face. He wished that he had somehow been able to rig a secret camera to record their reactions. What an absolute riot it would have been to study in slow motion their natural responses to his news.

"I came here because I love your daughter. I love her more than I love myself." He spoke as if on a meter. Three words at a time and with stoic gravitas, just as he had rehearsed while lying in bed the night before. "I can't imagine my life without your Shell, and I want her to be my wife. I'd like your blessing to ask her to marry me."

Dead silence ruled the table. Christie had started another pot of coffee just minutes earlier, and it was pouring out in a halting, unsteady stream.

"Leonard, this is such a surprise." It was Christie who spoke first, as Len had anticipated. "We knew you two were serious, but we just; I just didn't know you were ready to be *married*!" Her voice wavered.

Dean weighed in rather slowly, and in a measured manner, "Well, you know Leonard, the only thing Christie and I want in this world is for our girls to be happy. That's all we want. And if you can take care of our daughter and treat her like she deserves to be treated—if you can do that, then I guess that's all we can ask for."

After it was over, Len felt satisfied that the first part of his plan had been executed to perfection. He hadn't realized at the time, but during the entirety of this lengthy business his body had very nearly given in to rigor mortis. He consciously willed his muscles to release and felt his spine slip a little at the bottom. Then his shoulders followed, and a great relief washed over him. Finally he was relaxed.

Now the only thing left to do was the most difficult part: he had to convince Shell that marriage was the right choice. He had not anticipated this development before they left the city, and so he had no engagement ring. But Shell was a different kind of woman, and for once her precocious nature would work in his favor. Just as he knew the importance of her parents' approval, he also knew a ring would not be a priority for her. After the proposal and the engagement, he would go out and buy her a nice-sized stone.

The idea of the ring being visible to other men as a sign that Shell was taken appealed to Len very much. It would relieve that gnawing nervousness that plagued him when she was not in his sight. There was always the annoying thought that some sorry bastard might come along and convince her to leave him. The ring would at least give him a small reprieve from that preoccupation.

SHELL

※ ※ ※

Now that he found himself riding shotgun in this rather large and loud farm truck with his woman at the wheel, he felt secure that the marriage proposal would succeed. After about an hour on the road, they came to a bridge that yawned out lazily over a large body of water. More than fifteen years had passed since Shell was there last, but she felt a strange sense of recognition when they drove over the lake and into the quaint little town.

"That was Grand Lake o' the Cherokees," she explained, "and this town that we're entering now is called Grove. I haven't been here since I was a little girl."

"Great," said Len. "Now pull into that supermarket; I need to run in and grab something to drink."

"Why don't we just run through a fast food joint or something?" Shell was preoccupied with finding a spot on Spooklight Road when they still had plenty of daylight left. The idea of driving around on the darkened back roads without knowing the area did not appeal to her sensibilities in the least.

"It won't take me long at all, promise; just pull in right here and I'll run in and out before you even notice I'm gone." Len gestured for her to turn into the parking lot of a small grocery store.

She obliged by pulling in and putting the truck in park. She left the engine running, even though she felt certain Len would not be as quick as he promised. He slammed the door and moved across the parking lot at a fairly fast clip, almost a jog.

Maybe he really will make it quick, she thought. She turned the music up. This time Aretha was hooting, "*hoo, hoo, hoo, I'm added to your chain, chain, chain.*"

The Queen of Soul was muffled by the door as Shell stepped out and closed it behind her. She took a couple of long steps to stretch out her leg muscles. They hadn't been on the road all that long, but already she felt a little sore. She was beginning to think that maybe her entire body had given up and decided to fall apart. *Wrinkles, tired muscles, no sex drive... What's next, hot flashes? Jeez Louise.*

She put her arms up over her head and twisted her torso, looking over her right shoulder. Her arms fell to her sides and she let out a whoosh of air.

"Aw shit," she mumbled. The left front tire of the pickup was low. It hadn't gone completely flat, but it definitely was in need of air. She looked over and saw a gas station just a few hundred yards away. There was still no sign of Len. There was time enough to go air up the tire before he came back out. She knew they didn't have time to stop someplace in town for a repair.

She hopped in the truck, drove over to the gas station, and pulled the big truck right up close so that the front driver's side tire was next to the air pump. As she was filling the tire, Shell found the source of the slow leak: a nail had punctured the tire and gone all the way through its wall. She held the tip of the air hose against the nozzle on the tire with her left hand and gently placed the index finger of her right over the top of the nail. There was no air escaping that she could feel. No telling how long it had been there.

She decided then and there that she would just air up the tire and not say a word to Len about the nail. If he knew about it, there would be no debate. He would insist that they stop someplace for repair, and there was just no time for that. She reasoned that if the tire was in such bad shape, it would have already gone flat by now. She replaced the hose, screwed the cap back onto the tire nozzle, and jumped back in the truck, whipping it around in a doughnut to park right back in their original slot. *What luck*, Shell thought. She felt a little dishonest for not getting Len's opinion, but she already knew his solution and it was unacceptable. Besides, they were only about an hour away according to the map, and they still had at least two hours of daylight left.

Leonard came bounding out of the grocery store with a huge brown paper bag. He walked past the passenger's side door and set the bag in the bed of the pickup.

Shell turned to try and catch a glimpse of the bag's contents. "Don't look!" Len shouted as he jumped into his seat. "It's a *surprise!*"

He reached over and grabbed hold of Shell's hand. She turned her head slowly and saw real happiness in his eyes. He looked a little like he had the first time he sat down next to her and struck up a conversation. He was clearly excited.

"I think this will be a night neither of us will ever forget for the rest of our lives," he said, without a hint of embarrassment.

She steered the truck back to Highway 10, and they continued driving north. The orange yolk of the sun was now beginning to abandon its watch overhead and had already begun its downward slide to the hills off in the west. "I know we're supposed to turn east at some point," Shell told Len. She watched him pore over the upper right-hand section of the state map. "Keep an eye on the road signs so we don't get lost."

When they came to a four-way stop in the road, Shell looked over at Len again. "I really think I'm supposed to turn right here."

"No, no, the closest town to Spooklight Road on this map is called Zena, and the best way to get there is to continue on north and then take the interstate."

"Now, I know for sure that we aren't supposed to take the interstate," she said.

"It's been years since you've been anywhere near this place," Len told her "You said so yourself. So you don't know any better, plus I have the map. So just drive on."

She held the steering wheel straight between her hands and pressed down on the gas pedal, continuing on the road north. She had a very strong feeling they had missed the turn, but Len did indeed have the map. He was usually good with navigation, so she deferred.

After thirty minutes passed, she knew that they were lost. Even worse, they had driven into the country doldrums. An endless stretch of blacktop ran ahead, flanked by crooked lines of barbed wire fence that marked off hilled and rocky pastures, though they had not seen a single horse or cow since leaving Grove. Dirt roads spider-webbed out of sight, but she did not dare turn down any of those; they would have been bona fide lost then, with no hope of finding their way out.

Compounding their troubles, Shell felt the steering wheel begin to tug to one side. The truck was riding strange, as though one side of it was pulling the other. She knew the front tire was low again, but she dared not speak a word of it to Len. He had not yet noticed a problem, and he would be furious if he knew she had driven them out into the country on a bad tire. She was pretty angry with herself for that matter. What a ridiculous risk to take. She considered her options. They could turn around and try to get back to Grove. But that would never work; they would be riding on the rim by the time they got back. *Dad must have a spare in the back*, she thought. Shell began to pull over to the edge of the road.

"What are you doing?" Len asked, sitting up and looking around.

"I think we might have a flat," she said with only the slightest sting of guilt.

"Oh, sonofabitch, that's just fuckin' lovely."

"I see your good mood has taken a sudden turn for the hateful," she replied in a calm tone. "I thought you were all bubbles and daisies, Len, or you were just half an hour ago." She jumped out before he had a chance to reply.

"Well, pardon me if I'm not wet in the pants at the thought of being stranded out here beside the road with no phone signal and no civilization in sight," he spat out, disgusted with this turn of fortune. *This could very well be the end of all my plans*, he thought to himself. He walked around to the other side of the truck so he could evaluate the tire for himself. "Yep, right there. Look, it's got a nail in it," he said after a quick inspection.

Shell tried to feign surprise at his discovery. She was a horrible actor, but Leonard was distracted and missed her poor performance. "Should we put on the spare?" she asked.

As they stood considering the fate of the tire, the lower rim of the sun touched the tops of the trees in the distance. It seemed to melt the landscape into a furious pink and yellow firestorm.

"I don't know," said Len. "Hell, I wouldn't be surprised if the spare was flat, too. We just *had* to take your dad's piece of shit truck, didn't we? It just wouldn't do to take our own vehicle, oh no, it had to be the Jethro truck. I knew something like this would happen."

Shell stood watching him throw his tantrum for a moment and then looked away at their surroundings. Even this far out in the country it was unusual that not a single car had passed while they were on the road checking the tire. The autumn breeze picked up, and she felt the warmth of the sun's rays falling away. A chill ran up her spine and over her scalp. She felt her hair stand on end, and she hoped that Len would hurry. The plans to reach Spooklight Road were in large part forgotten. The major concern now was to get off the road before night came.

"Let's just drive until we get to a town with a tire place," Len said. He got back into the truck, but in the driver's seat this time, and they continued on down the road, looking off in the distance for any lights that might herald a place to stop.

After five miles or so, Shell spotted a single yellow light burning from a window up ahead. The car's headlights brought a rusted white sign into view, hanging next to a rundown, whitewashed brick building. The sign was in the shape of a horizontal diamond; it had once heralded the brand of a long-since defunct oil company. It was painted over now and hung from a pole with peeling red letters that read, *Zeke's Tire & Tow*. Rust ran down the face of it in blurry orange lines, following the rain streams brought by heavy storms.

She never saw rust without the old Neil Young lyric, "rust never sleeps," cycling through her head; it was an involuntary reaction by now.

They pulled up outside. Len threw the gear shift into park, and they sat motionless with the engine idling, both staring straight ahead.

"You want me to go in there?" Shell asked. When she thought back to her last incident with a gas station attendant, her mouth pulled up into an automatic snarl. She could not believe Len hadn't already volunteered to go inside.

"It's embarrassing," he said. "You're the one who wanted to set out on this trip to begin with and besides you have a way with these…locals, for lack of a better word, that I don't have. They look at me and see a Yankee Red. You grew up around here.

They like you; they like your accent. They'd probably just as soon shoot me as talk to me."

"That would be an absolute travesty," she whispered under her breath as she stepped out of the car. She walked up the rocky grade of an embankment toward the front door of the building. The place looked like an old garage. She figured it to be at least sixty years old. Shell reached the door and paused. She wasn't frightened per se, just somewhat uneasy. People in these parts did not appreciate unannounced visitors, particularly not late at night.

Bong, bong, bong, BONG, her four knocks on the door echoed on the metal. She hadn't meant to hit with that kind of force; the echo made her knock sound like she was beating down the door. She heard some tinkering inside come to an abrupt halt.

"We're *closed.*" A gnarled, deep voice called out from behind the door.

"I—*we*—need some help. Please, sir," she said in her most helpless voice, hoping to convince the angry person inside that she meant no harm.

A rusted lock turned and squeaked, and suddenly the door swung in by about a foot. The yellow light inside surrounded a tall old man, clothed in blue-and-white striped overalls. Their color made Shell think of a train conductor. He must have been in his sixties, standing there in the doorway with a quizzical expression on his bearded face. His white beard was braided down the front and hung halfway down his midsection. In his right hand he held a heavy tool of some kind; she guessed it was a giant wrench.

"Oh, Jesus," she said, startled. The words slipped out before she had a chance to catch them, and she immediately felt regret. Taking the lord's name in vain could be a serious offense out here in God's country.

"I mean gosh, I'm so sorry to bother you," she said. "We've been driving around on a low tire, and we're lost. Haven't seen a gas station for miles, and your place was the only one we've seen in over half an hour. We were worried we might get stranded out here in the dark."

The old man looked past Shell at the truck. He seemed suspicious of her story.

"This ain't no business."

"But your sign says…"

"Don't matter what that sign says, Miss. *I'm* tellin' you I ain't no *business*. Haven't had a customer here in thirty years. This is my own shop. I work on my own vehicles here. Nobody else's."

"I understand, and I'm so sorry I bothered you," she said, "but we don't have anywhere else to go. Do you think you can help us? I have plenty of cash, and I'll pay you double the cost."

"I don't work for pay," he said, and although his voice remained low and serious, his heavy eyelids rose a little along with his eyebrows, as though he only now really saw her for the first time. His features softened, and she felt an ease in the tension between them. He held out his hand.

"Name's Zeke." She reached out to shake his hand, but he only took the tips of her fingers in his grasp and lightly bounced her hand up and down. Len had been right about that part. She did have a way with men— a way of disarming them, perhaps.

"What are you doing way out here on this road, anyway? Don't nobody drive down this road 'cept the folks left livin' out here. Not many of them, neither. Ever'body else takes Highway 69, or the interstate. We don't get traffic down this road. Haven't for thirty-some-odd years."

A little reddish-brown puppy came running up from the back of the building.

"Some watchdog you are, Leo," Zeke said, reaching down to scratch the dog's head. Zeke's hands were huge and covered over with calluses and scars. His fingernails needed trimming, and they curved downward over the ends of his fingers. They were stained yellow with nicotine.

"Soon as you pulled up, he ran to the back," said Zeke. "Came roaming up here a week or so ago, scared shitless. Scared of everything, even the wind. Guess some asshole took to beatin' him, then got tired of that too and threw him out for trash."

Shell couldn't figure why this old man was telling her his dog's life story, but she was patient. She could wait as long as needed if it meant getting the tire fixed. Maybe after he was through talking, he would help. He happened to be the only option at the moment, and the words of her mother came flashing through like a neon sign: 'beggars can't be choosers, Shell.'"

The old man continued Leo's story: "Tried to run him off, but he just kept hangin' around outside. Finally got sick of fightin' him off, and just let him in. Sometimes that happens, you know; you just get sick and tired and give in to something you don't want to do. Somethin' you shouldn't be responsible for."

Good Lord, maybe this old guy is certifiable, Shell thought. Her eyes followed the path to the door, just in case she had to make a quick break for it.

"He seems like a sweet little dog," Shell said, forcing a smile. She reached out her hand. Leo showed her his teeth in a silent, half-hearted growl, then ducked his head and ran under the workbench.

"He don't like people much," said Zeke. "'Cept me, I guess. Ain't natural for a dog to be scared of people. Dogs is supposta love people."

Outside, the truck horn blared three times. Shell jumped, startled.

"What you nervous for, Missy?" Zeke asked, "Better go out there and tell that feller to lay off the horn 'less he wants to get his own bell rung."

Shell turned and sprinted outside to the truck, where Len was waiting with his head stuck outside the window.

"Fuckin' hell," Len said. "What's going on in there? I thought maybe you'd been knocked on the head and strung up by your ankles!"

"So what, you were just going to sit out here and let me hang?"

He smiled and looked down, "Ah shit, I didn't think you were really in trouble. I coulda heard you scream out here if you were. Just trying to get you to make it snappy is all. What are you two doing in there anyway? Trading services, or what?" He snorted at his little joke.

She ignored the snide remark and said, "I think that guy is going to help us. He seems like he will, anyway. He's just a big talker," she said, looking back at the building. She decided not to tell Len about Zeke's promise to ring his bell. "I think he must be awful lonesome. He's been telling me all about his dog. Just wait out here; everything's fine. As soon as he's done talking, I'm sure he'll patch up the tire and we can get going." She turned to walk back up the short embankment to the door.

"Shell!" Leonard called out after her.

"*Jeez*, Len, what *is* it?" she hissed back.

"Hurry the hell up."

She rolled her eyes and strode back inside. When she walked in again, she noticed that Zeke had quite a penchant for pin-up girls. All plastered along the west wall of the shop were old posters of fleshy women: Betty Grable, Eartha Kitt, Jayne Mansfield. He obviously had a thing for legs, because every pose featured a shapely set of them. They covered the entirety of his wall, a jumble of legs lined up alongside, and on top of, each other. *Giant wall o' gams*, she thought to herself. *ZZ Top would feel right at home in this place.*

Zeke followed her gaze and said sheepishly, "I don't get many women in here, Miss. Spend most of my time here by myself. Every once in a while one of the guys drops by. But no women. Sorry for that; I hope you aren't offended by my ladies."

Shell was charmed to realize that this rough and worn old guy had turned shy in front of her.

"Oh, please," she reassured him. "You'll have to do a whole lot worse than that to offend a girl like me."

Zeke's face registered relief, and then he quickly changed the subject.

"Now did you ever answer my question?" he asked.

"Which one, sir?"

"I told you, it's Zeke."

"Which one, Zeke?"

"The one about what you're doing way out here in the middle of nowhere. This ain't no place for a young lady to be running around, getting lost and having flats on the side the road."

"We have a map," Shell said, "but maybe some of these roads aren't on it or something. I'm not sure. I was trying to find Spooklight Road. I know it's around here pretty close. There isn't a town anywhere near the place, and you have to kind of luck your way onto it down a bunch of back roads."

Zeke reached over to lay the wrench down, and then walked to a giant wooden crate that sat on a palate filled with a sea of old tools and cords. He bent over, rummaging around inside with his back to her. He began to speak without looking up.

"You're in the general area to find it," he said. "But I wouldn't advise you to go looking for the damned thing." His tone was nonchalant. "If you don't know what you're doin', or where you're goin', you might find yourself in a whole heap of trouble real quick."

"Not too many things worse than being lost in these parts," he continued, raising his voice without giving her a chance to reply. "Harden. You ever heard of a town called Harden?" He stopped rummaging in the crate and cranked his neck around to look at Shell.

"Uh, no sir, I don't think I have." She was beginning to lose her patience. Did her new-found friend expect her to stay the rest of the night and listen to a primer on small town Oklahoma history?

"It's a town," he went on, "or used to be a town anyway. It's right up the road from here. I've heard people say that what went on up there had something to do with that light you're talking about. Never seen it myself. Never went lookin' for it neither. But anyway, as the story goes, back before the first war that little town, Harden, it looked just like the rest of the four-state convergence. Craggy old rocky fields. Couldn't hardly grow a thing in the A farmer named Rogers owned the land there. This old guy let some people out on his land to do some surveying, and they came back and told him he had a shitload of lead and zinc ore under his place. He was sittin' on a million tons of the stuff. So in other words, y'see, what he was sittin' on was a giant pile of money."

Zeke shifted his weight from one foot to the other, shoved his hands deep in the pockets of his overalls, and leaned back against the wall next to his tool crate.

"Well," he said, "this mining outfit, they offered him a sum of money larger than he'd ever heard of in his life, except in fairy tales—a hundred thousand times more than he'd ever *had* in his life, and they bought the place right out from under him.

"Of course," Zeke said, "the stuff under that worthless old field was worth a million times more than even that. Before you could turn around—I mean *overnight*—this patch of rocky pasture became a mining town. They named the place after the owner of the company. Harden. You probably could'a guessed that part." He paused, waiting on a reaction from his solo audience.

Shell obliged him with a nod to carry on, and he did: "All that time, up until forty years or so ago, that place was just a regular old town—alive and bustling, you see. But the whole time, the mining company was up underneath the surface, tunneling. They cut giant shafts right out from under the residential areas that had been built for the miners and their families; I mean, they literally pulled the carpet right out from under their feet.

"And of course, all of the earth they tore out, all of that dirt, why they weren't gonna stuff it back into those holes—not while there was more money in there waitin' to be drug out. So they just piled the chat around everywhere—that's what the mining waste is called, Missy, *chat* piles—they piled it next to the creek where the kids went to swim every summer, built up a few mounds of it behind the school and the local church. Hell, even city hall could open a window and flip a quarter onto a chat pile if they wanted."

"Most of the people in the town had no idea what was going on, and the mining company intended to keep it that way, too. The ore and stuff they took out of the ground—why, they left scraps of it in big piles. When it rained, all that metal ran off into the groundwater, contaminated it. And this was some nasty stuff. The kind of stuff'd make your kids grow an extra limb or three, you know what I mean?"

Shell nodded. She really just wanted him to get on with it.

"But do you know, that ain't really the worst part? I mean, maybe it is for some, but to me, the worst part was what the mining did to that town. They tore up the earth underneath. Hundreds of tunnels in the ground below. Made kind of like a honeycomb of the ground beneath all the buildings." His eyes narrowed as he spoke. "And turned that place into quicksand."

Shell laughed nervously. "Oh, come on," she said. "That can't be right."

"Yes'm, it is. Some places where there was plenty of water, the soil turned to quicksand. Some parts just opened up into huge sinkholes where entire houses and the people in 'em was just swallowed up whole, into the earth. It's a ghost town now," he went on. "I mean a *ghost* town. Not a person left in there. Environmental folks from the government came in, shut the entire area down. Blocked it off. But there are still ways to get in. So, after the mining company came in and made their money off the land—it took 'em a few decades to really squeeze out every last drop—they just picked up their toys and left. Didn't clean a damn spec of it up. Didn't warn nobody that their homes were just one gulley washer away from a first class mudslide ticket straight to hell."

"Government came in several years later and tested all the kids in town. Guess what? Poisoned. Nearly every single last one of those babies that grew up around Harden had a big ol' dose of lead flowing through their veins. The heavy metal generation. Sounds funny, 'cept it ain't."

"So it's actually been declared a Superfund site?" Shell asked, genuinely interested at last.

"Not a damn thing super or fun about it." He delivered the line, deadpan.

Shell scanned his face to see if maybe he was making a joke (*He must be making a joke*, she thought), but she found no sign of amusement there, so she didn't say a word. There was a pause, and she thought he must surely be finished. She was wrong.

"Then," he said, "four years ago one of the largest tornadoes to ever pass through this state plowed right through the middle of Harden. Tore everything up, whatever was left, just like you threw a box of toothpicks into a blender. I guess the people who stay here and try to live on, just like Old Rogers back before the war, why they're either cursed or crazy. Maybe both. It's not just about the mine, either.

"The Indians knew this place was cursed when they first set foot on the land when coming through on the Trail. They just kept on walking past, fast as they could. Kept moving south 'til they got to

Tahlequah. So I'm tellin' you, God hates this place, or at least He hates what the people who lived here before done to it. And the people who live around here now, why most of them hate it just as much as God does. But cain't none of us leave."

Shell refrained from asking any more questions. Zeke's face had become flushed, and his calloused hands had doubled up in fists while he spoke. "What I'm tryin' to get you to see here is, folks like you don't belong in these parts. You ought not be out driving around these little towns and back roads on your own, looking for something that ain't lost and don't need to be found. Lots of tricks and trap falls waiting around this land. It's all waitin' on you to wander right into a hole. There are some things you wouldn't even believe or understand, callin' out for people to go lookin' for sights no man ought to see, just waitin' to swaller you up whole. Consume you with fire."

For the first time since she knocked on the door, Shell felt frightened. She wasn't scared of Zeke, but she thought back to the bird that flew into her house, and to the dead man's eye on the road. She thought about the perverted man at the convenience store, and about all of her problems with Len. Hadn't these been warning signs—stop signs even, screaming for her to turn around? Now here was the culmination of it all, in this strange man who spoke of destruction with all the cheery delivery of Revelation.

Zeke saw the fear written on her face and took a step toward her. "Just don't get hurt, Missy; I didn't mean to upset you. You just need to be careful, is all." He paused a beat and then returned to the business of their tire: "Now go on out and tell your feller to drive the truck in here. I'll go pull up the door, and we'll get you fixed right up so you can head on back home. Hey, you wanna know something else about Harden?"

There's no end to this, she thought to herself.

"What?" she asked aloud, on the verge now of losing her composure.

"One of them Rascal Flatts, you heard of them, that country singin' band? One of them boys comes from Harden."

"Well, then it's no wonder God has forsaken the place," Shell replied with a mischievous light in her eye. At first she feared he might be put off by her sarcasm, but he grabbed the front of his belt with both hands and bent over laughing. She could still hear his guffaws when the door swung shut behind her. She walked out to the truck and found that Len was nowhere to be seen.

"*Len*, where are you? *Hello!*" She cupped both hands to her mouth, strained her neck forward, and yelled into the darkness as loud as she could.

"Hey, come back here," his voice sounded tiny, and she knew he was back behind Zeke's shop.

Len had decided to relieve his bladder out back behind the building. He couldn't believe how quickly night had descended on them. The sky was dark and black. He couldn't see a single star in the sky, or any sign of the moon for that matter. *Must be a storm blowing in,* he thought as he negotiated the rocky terrain to find a good pissing spot.

Shell heard the crunch of his footsteps returning, but she didn't wait for him to get back around. She jumped into the driver's seat and started the engine. As Zeke raised the garage door, the yellow light from his shop tumbled out of the widening space at the bottom of the door. She waited for him to give the signal and then slowly inched the truck forward until the entire front end was inside. The shop was too full of junk to drive the rest of the way in.

Len walked in through the side door as Zeke was putting the truck up on a jack.

"Was that your idea of a funny trick? Going out back to hide?" Shell asked.

"Just went back there to take a whiz," he replied.

Zeke was using a tire iron to loosen the big lugs on the truck tire. They must have been put on extremely tight, because he had to lean his massive body weight over the tool just to get the lugs to loosen. His mood was markedly different now, and it was obvious he no longer cared about trading stories or making friends. Shell gave Len a look that told him to shut up, and he did.

Zeke finished patching the tire and released the jack. After he removed the nail from the tire, he held it up and looked at Shell. He dropped the jack, and the right front side of the pickup dropped a few inches. The frame bobbed a couple of times before coming to rest.

"Now listen, both of you: I just put a temporary patch on that tire. It won't last any time at all. So don't go driving down any more gravel roads or running these state highways around here. For that matter, you better keep it at fifty or below. Any faster and you're likely to blow that tire. Just drive from here straight back to Miami." He pronounced the name of the town *Miamuh*. "You'll find a couple of shops in town that can put a used tire on there. That'll get you the rest of the way home."

He turned to Shell. "Hey Missy," he added, "before you go, you better take my card. Just in case you ever find yourself stranded again." She felt certain Zeke must be joking. The idea of this strange, lonely man handing out business cards struck her as absurd. But indeed, he was digging something out of an old red-and-black Velcro wallet. He pulled out a warped piece of rectangular paper and handed it to her. Shell stuck the card in the hip pocket of her jeans without reading it.

"I can't thank you enough," she said. "I don't know what we would have done, stranded out here with no phone signal." A moment of hesitation hung in the air between the two, and then she realized that she hadn't paid him.

"Oh!" She was embarrassed and afraid that their good samaritan would think she was trying to get away without paying for his help. Len looked over to see what she was harping about. Shell bolted to the truck and flung open the door. It swung out and knocked into the wooden crate with a loud bang. "I forgot to pay you!"

As she reached inside and grabbed a twenty out of the wallet in her purse, she felt Zeke grab her wrist. She was startled by it. His touch carried a jolt of electricity; she felt a surge of power course through her body. He must have experienced the same shock, because he released his grip almost as soon as he grabbed hold of her.

"Please," he said. "Don't worry about the money. All I did was patch the tire. That don't cost a thing. I don't want to hear another word about it."

Shell wanted to protest. She hated the feeling of owing a favor—it was one of her greatest hang-ups. But she saw in his face that he would not be moved, so she allowed herself to remain in his debt without an argument.

She opened her mouth to gush another thank you, but he interrupted. "Go on now," he said. "It's late. Go on home." With these last words, Shell could see an inexplicable sorrow in his eyes.

He must feel so alone out here, she thought.

She could not shake the feeling that by leaving that shop they were leaving safe refuge. Her annoyed impatience with Zeke's strange conversation was gone, and now she was fascinated. *What else does he know that he didn't say?* she wondered.

"All ready to go?" Len popped back in to her consciousness. She'd nearly forgotten that he was still there.

"Yep, sure," she said in a rush, throwing a glance over at Zeke. He seemed to have lost all interest in them, and was off tinkering with a ratchet as if they were already long gone. Once they backed out of the garage and turned out on the road, Shell pulled the card out from her pocket and reached up to flip on the interior light. His business card was worn smooth with age. She had to hold it up right in front of her face and squint to make out the words. The card read:

Ezekiel's Wheels
Get your wheels back on the road in a FLASH!
73113 Hwy 69 South
Quapaw, Oklahoma 74363
(918) 304-5554

Chapter 11

Shell

> *You gotta make it your own way, but you'll be all right now, sugar.*
> Guns N' Roses, "Don't Cry"

"Good God, what was *that* about?" Len asked, laughing.

Shell giggled too, happy to be rid of the tension that had boiled up between Len and the strange old man. "Len, have you ever in your life even heard of anything as crazy as these last two days?"

Before he could answer, Shell shook her head in disbelief, "To tell the truth, it's all starting to get old now. Enough with the car crashes and the perverted cashiers and apocalyptic mechanics. I'm just ready now for a healthy dose of normal."

"You're the one who dreamt up this big idea," he reminded her again, sounding a little distracted. He sat there in the driver's seat, looking one way down the highway and then the other. He turned the truck back south.

"Why are we going back this way?" She asked.

"Don't you think we may as well just take the truck back to your parents for the night? Save your Dad a trip and get his truck back to him."

She'd expected to go straight on the interstate to make the four-hour drive to the city. She considered his explanation for a moment before saying, "I suppose we ought to. That guy did say we shouldn't go over fifty miles per hour. They'll be surprised to see us back tonight. And without any news about the Spooklight. Oh well." She shrugged, feeling more exhausted than dejected. "At least Dad will be pleased we never made it to Spooklight Road, won't he?"

Len let her words hang in the air between them unacknowledged. He was thinking still. Pissed off as he had been, their little diversion off course could be used to add a new element of surprise to his plans. Earlier she'd suspected him of treachery, but now she had forgotten all about that, and thought they were driving away from Spooklight Road back toward her parents' home. This way she would be even more shocked and delighted by his proposal. A smirk of self-satisfaction teased its way across his mouth, unnoticed by Shell.

When they reached the four-way stop they had passed when travelling north, Len made a left-hand turn, headed east. This was the one divergence where, he feared, she might start asking questions. He looked over at her after the truck straightened out again, and saw that she was lost in a daydream again, staring out the window at the passing scenery. It annoyed him most of the time, because it meant she was not listening. But now he was grateful that she failed to pay attention to their direction.

Leonard had driven just under twenty miles when he saw it: a large wooden sign made of split logs. The faded white paint on it read *DEVIL'S PROMENADE*. A makeshift arrow pointed down the dark dirt road running off to the north. Len felt a jolt of satisfaction. Shell still didn't know that he had looked up a little information of his own the night before, specifically regarding how to reach Spooklight Road. He continued east on the blacktop past one, then two, more side roads. At the second one, he turned the wheel to his left and once again they were going north. Now Shell snapped to attention.

"Where are we going?"

"We're on Spooklight Road," Len replied, his face alight in excitement.

"How did you know..." she trailed off, staring ahead.

"I did a little research last night while you were up talking to your folks," he said, trying to mask his glee. It was all coming together better than he imagined. Even the unplanned detours worked in his favor. This night was meant to be, he thought; the plot of it written long ago. He imagined the story of their engagement would be repeated to their children and grandchildren for years to come.

He thought the drive would be much farther off the state highway, but altogether they only had to travel two and a half miles off the blacktop before they arrived at a little lane that branched off to the left.

Shell was shocked to see that a road sign, just like the one on neighborhood streets, stood at the intersection. Anyplace else it might have read Rambling Oaks Drive or Elmwood Place. This sign read Spooklight Road.

Just seeing the words sent a thrilled little shiver of excitement down her spine. She felt just like she had all those years ago, as she sat beside the campfire, her mind on fire with the images of a black panther, an alien visitor, and the Loch Ness monster all swimming around in a fantastic mystery stew.

She was no longer angry at Leonard for taking her out here. This was, after all, the entire reason for the trip, and they would have been stupid to disregard their plans because of a bad tire. She stared down the dark lane for any sign of a light.

"The site I looked at said we're supposed to drive until we see a low-water bridge," said Len. "Then pull over to the side of the road and turn out the lights on the truck. We're supposed to watch that rise in the road up ahead. That's where the light should to appear."

Len drove ahead at twenty miles per hour so they could watch for the low-water bridge. They both spotted it at the same time, as the headlights brought the flat cement into view. It had been a dry fall, and the little creek that sometimes spilled over it had dried up weeks before. He pulled over and put the truck in park, then cut the engine.

"Well, babe," he said, "here we are."

Shell had a broad smile across her face. "You found it, Len. Thank you!" She threw open her door, jumped out, and walked to the front of the truck. Leonard stayed inside for a moment and watched her lean back against the warm grill and stretch her elbows back onto the hood for support.

He stepped out and gently shut the door, trying to avoid making too much sound. He walked to the back of the truck and grabbed the bundle that he'd placed there earlier in the day. He rummaged around and pulled out a soft chenille blanket and a five-foot-long piece of foam. *It's just right out here*, he thought, *to sit and talk.*

He found an even spot in the middle of the low-water bridge and placed the foam on the ground with the blanket on top. Shell straightened up to see what he was doing.

"You brought a pallet out here?" she asked.

He reached down with his hand and patted a spot on the foam for her to sit down on.

She laughed nervously. "What if a car comes?"

"Look around," he said. "There isn't a soul around here for miles and miles. It's just the two of us."

She did not want to disappoint him; he had made such an effort to get here. After all the things he had said, taunting her about the Spooklight idea, now he was going to make up for it all. She felt guilty for all the times she snapped at him over the past two days. He really wasn't such a bad guy; at least he was trying. She sat down in the spot he indicated and looked up. She could see the sparkle in his eyes even in the darkness.

"Just wait right here," he said.

"What in the world are you doing?"

"There's more. Just wait, okay?"

She settled in her spot and kept her eyes ahead. Len was back at the truck again, rustling around. A light came on behind her, and she turned to see him with a basket in his arms and a flashlight in one hand.

She began to suspect that this was no midnight picnic. "Len, you have to turn out the light and be quiet. I told you we can't make any noise."

He ignored her request and set the wicker basket down on the blanket beside her. When he pulled back the edge of the cloth that covered the basket's contents, she saw it was full of goodies.

The first thing he took out was a bottle of champagne. He must have had it chilling in the ice chest in the back of the truck. It was a bottle of Dom. The flashlight was lying on the ground behind them, and it cast an arc of light just over the top of the basket.

Len took two champagne flutes from a couple of handkerchiefs and sat them up on the cement next to their pallet. He popped the cork and filled them almost to the top, then he took out a little bowl and removed the lid. Freshly cut strawberries were inside, and he dropped one into each glass.

She wondered how and when he'd found time to dream all of this up. It was a bit much and all but ruined her plans to sit and watch in silence.

Len handed her the flute closest to her and picked up his own. He raised it in the air and gestured for her to do the same.

"Shell Georgene Foster," he began, in a somber tone that indicated he had already planned a grand speech for the occasion.

Shell's eyebrows shot up as she realized that this was not just some casual memorialization of their first time on Spooklight Road. Could he be... Oh no, surely he wasn't going to propose out here. Her thoughts raced back to the night before, when her sister had told her she should talk to him about their relationship at the first opportunity. "Do it tonight," she had said. Now Shell regretted, with every synapse firing in her brain, that she had not taken that advice. Once again, she could see that her own cowardice was leading them both in a direction she did not want to travel.

Len continued, saying, "I never told you about the first time I saw you. It wasn't that day when we first spoke at the union. It was two days before. I was walking past and saw you sitting there. I didn't even see your face, Shell. I could only see you from behind. Your dark hair and your long legs. The way you sat there, all alone and confident, with your book and your messy hair. I know it's hard to believe right now, but I swear in that moment I knew we would be together. I waited for you there the next day. All day I sat in the union hoping to find you again, but you never showed. I thought I'd lost you; that I'd somehow missed out on my destiny."

He hesitated for a moment, feeling sheepish for the first time at the length of his speech. He saw that Shell was uneasy. Her body was tense, as though she was considering the notion of running off in the dark. He wondered if he should have thought of something better to say, but it was too late to take it back now.

"Since that second day," he said, "when you spoke to me, I've known you were the one—the only woman I would ever spend the rest of my life with."

Shell felt her eyes widen another millimeter and thought they might fall right out of their sockets and into her lap. She started to speak again, but Leonard would not have it just yet.

"I realized in the last couple of days that we have taken so much for granted," he said. "We shouldn't waste another day, Shell."

He rose up from his sitting position and balanced himself on one knee.

"Marry me, Shell."

She sat there, with her mouth formed in the perfect shape of an O, for what seemed like five minutes, unable to speak or move. Her mind raced, searching for a response; for some way to break the news to him without causing pain. But even then, she was coming to terms with the brutal revelation. *Not this time*, a voice inside her said. *This time you have to tell the truth.*

She cleared her throat to speak and found her throat dry. The champagne was the only liquid around, so she picked up the flute and took a big swallow, downing half of the glass in one swig. Len laughed nervously, thinking it was her attempt at a joke.

"Listen, Len," she started, then stopped again, struggling for the proper words, "I do love you, and I always will, no matter what happens."

A giant smile crossed his face, and she realized with genuine horror that he had no idea what she was about to say.

"This isn't going to work," she blurted out.

Len's countenance darkened, and the smile dropped right off his face. Shell thought it was much like a thunderstorm that blew a sudden mass of black clouds in to overtake a blue summer sky.

His eyebrows, which had been raised in anticipation of her answer, dropped to a furrowed line. There was a look of confusion and hurt in his eyes. It was the startled look of a wounded animal.

She waited for a reply, but none came. He dropped her left hand, which he had taken when he began the proposal.

The clouds were moving overhead, and the dim light of the crescent moon illuminated a tiny space in their midst. Shell studied the sky and found that she could not tell the difference between the dark and the light. The clouds and the sky were a bleak mosaic of gray and charcoal shading. When he spoke at last, his voice was choked and shaking with emotion: "Why would you do this to me?" he asked.

"We haven't been happy together," Shell said. "You know that."

"Do you know anybody who feels happy all the time, Shell? Do you know people who agree on every little fucking thing and never, ever fight?"

"That isn't the point, Len"

Then *what is the point?*" he yelled. His pain was transformed to anger by a perceived flippancy in her voice.

The intensity of his reaction startled her.

"Could you please explain the fucking point," Len said, "because, as you can see, I just don't get it!" He continued, "We've been together for three years. I gave up my future in Boston for you. I left my friends and my parents behind to stay here in this backwoods, hillbilly, shit hole just to be with *you*, Shell. And you never said a word in protest. You sat back and let me do it!"

"Len, I never asked you to do those things for me," she said in a whisper.

"But you sure as hell didn't tell me not to, did you?" he demanded. "Did you plan this all along? Was this an amusing experiment for you, to see just how wicked you could mind-fuck a man and then let him go? How long have you felt this way?"

"It's not that easy," she said. "I don't know how long I've felt like this. I've known for a while, I guess." Shell knew the truth would cause him to become even angrier, but there was no need to dance around it. The time of reckoning had come, and she had her own blame to bear in this mess.

"Why did you bring me here?" Leonard demanded, his voice breaking with emotion. "Did you plan to break the news that my life with you was a complete fuck up, out here in the middle of a black wasteland, so nobody else would see how cruel and sick you really are? Do you have any *idea* just how cruel you are?"

"You know that's not true," said Shell. "You wanted to come with me. I didn't make you come here. You're upset, Len; please calm down. It doesn't have to be like this."

Len stood and crossed his arms over his chest, looking down at her as though Shell were some kind of revolting insect.

"Doesn't have to be like *what?*" he demanded. "Just tell me now, Shell, since it looks like you have all the power and all the answers. You're in control, just like always, aren't you? You want me to calm down. Act like you. But look at you. Do you even have feelings like most human beings? You just told the person you've lived with for the last three years that you don't want to see him anymore, and there you sit. Dry as a bone. Not even a hint of a tear. You're cold, Shell. You're one cold bitch."

She winced at the word. She was accustomed to their arguments, and plenty of curse words to boot, but not this name-calling. Until now, he'd never demeaned her. Shell felt threatened now. The only response she knew was to keep her own voice at a measured, calm level and hope that it would ratchet down the intensity.

"It doesn't have to be ugly," she pleaded, "I meant what I said before. I do love you; I love you as a person and I love you as a…"

Her calm approach only infuriated him further.

"Don't you say it!" He screamed. His eyes were wild and rolling; much more white could be seen than usual, and spit sprayed from his mouth when he spoke. Fury lived in his face, unchecked. "Don't you dare say what you're thinking right now. I'm right on the edge here, Shell, and if you say you love me like a fucking friend, I'm telling you, I don't know what I'll do."

She wondered what he could mean by that. He was not a violent person. He couldn't mean he wanted to hurt her.

"But I don't understand why, after all this time together," she continued, "why we can't still care about each other and wish each other well. We *are* friends. I don't see why that part has to go away."

"You couldn't do it, could you? Couldn't keep your mouth shut. Well, here's news for you. You aren't my friend," he snarled. "You are the enemy. In fact, even my worst enemy would never have brought me here to spit in my face and dispose of me like a piece of trash. As if I never meant a thing to you. As if the last three years of my life amount to nothing."

With that, Leonard kicked his foot out at the champagne bottle. It fell over, spilling its contents across the blanket and shattering her glass on the cement.

"I hope you have fun out here with your sick little games and your crazy fucking ghost light."

She kept quiet and looked up at him, unsure what to say now. He turned and walked back to the truck and got in, started the engine and smashed the gas pedal with a roar.

Shell stood up, frightened now that she realized he could very easily run her down. Her instinct said he would never, but it was best not to play chicken with a farm truck. She took a step back, to the very edge of the cement ledge of the bridge.

Len slammed the truck into drive and turned the steering wheel hard. He rammed it forward and it smashed into the ditch. She heard the crunch of the grill as it ground into the rocks. Then he put the truck in reverse and backed up, spraying gravel over Shell and the pallet.

She watched helplessly as he completed a frantic five-point turn in the middle of the road, then gunned the pickup back in the opposite direction. The red brake lights flickered for a brief moment, and then he was gone.

※ ※ ※

Len's fury rose with his speed. It flowed and melded itself together into a sparking fire of energy that burned for Shell alone. He had no idea where he was going, or why he'd left her alone out there in the dark. He was operating on autopilot; now the reigns were handed over to some off-kilter auto-internal jockey who was more than happy to take over.

How could she? he kept asking himself over and over again. He was through considering her point of view. Everything he had done that night—and for the past three years, for that matter—had been for her. And now he found himself in a stolen pickup, rumbling down an abandoned dirt road with the woman he loved left behind in the dust. He had to admit a real sense of satisfaction had come when the truck sprayed Shell with gravel and dust, as if with just that one act of carelessness he'd regained a small piece of control and pride, which she had fileted so easily.

He saw that the truck was approaching a curve in the road much faster than anticipated, and he slammed on the brakes. Len felt the wheels swing out from under him, just for a second, and then he was back in control again. He slowed down some. *I don't have a death wish,* he thought, and then, *She'd probably be relieved if I just died out here on the road.*

A cacophony of imaginary voices called out for his attention. One cried out for justice. Another demanded revenge. And there was a voice that screamed in sorrow, loudest of all, that Shell was gone forever; it was all over. The smallest of them whispered that he could make it all okay if he would stop and be still, calm down. If he thought about Shell back there alone, it said, he could realize the truth in her words, regardless of the pain they carried.

But the hurricane of the other voices overcame the smallest, and Leonard Harris drove on blindly without any sense of reason or hope. He saw the wooden sign he'd noticed on the way to Spooklight Road. He felt driven to turn in the direction of its arrow, so he did. He found himself moving down another dark dirt road. There was a sense that he should turn around, but some engine within drove him on toward the location named by the sign. In the madness of the night, he just wanted to find someplace and stop. His head was a swirling fugue and, in the midst of it all, Len wanted to make it stop.

Up ahead, a clearing came into view of the headlights. It was a horseshoe-shaped area that looked out onto the river below. Leonard was not interested in sight-seeing, but he figured it was the only place off the road where he could settle down and determine his next move.

When he swung his legs out of the truck, the muscles in his arms and legs screamed out in protest. They were seized up in knots, as though he had just been in a fist fight. When he finally sat down out on the giant rock, he focused on releasing the tension that gripped his body. It began with his toes and progressed to his calves. When his shoulders gave way and released their spasm, he felt a deep relief and an immediate sense of regret.

Tears ran freely down his cheeks and onto the rock beneath him. "How did this happen?" he cried out. The words caused him to jump a little when they echoed back to him from the valley below.

So this is it, he thought. *It's all over now. The entire dream gone, in the span of less than an hour.* He put his head in his hands and wept. The sound of his sobs echoing back up made him feel all the more pathetic.

His fingers were clamped over his eyes, as though shielding them from the cruel sight of the world around him. Without warning, a stab of light penetrated the tiny space between his first two fingers. Then came another, and now his cupped hands were full of a great shining luminescence. He hesitated to look up, fearing someone stood there with a flashlight. He was ashamed to have been discovered in this place, sobbing alone in the dark. What possible explanation could he give?

When he took his hands away and lifted his gaze, the sight before him was unlike any he had ever known. There before him was an unnatural glowing orb of light, a beautiful illuminated night-emerald suspended in the air. His first thought was sorrow, for Shell had missed out on her Spooklight. And he had found it right here on the ledge of Devil's Promenade. Part of him wanted to turn and run for the shelter of the truck, but another one, the stronger of the two, demanded he stand and look into the light.

When he gazed at its brilliance, his body felt a sudden shock and he staggered back. A grisly movie flashed through his mind, made up of every memory he'd ever wanted to forget; events he hated and had never wanted to revisit. But there they were, undeniable, burning and taunting his mind.

There was the grinning maw of his father's bloody mouth as he stood over the sink, reeking of gin. So too was the sight of a starving puppy kicked in the ribs by his buddies, until it whined and lay down, too weak to run away. Shell's outline was there too, her back turned away as she disappeared in the crowd. His own image was next, sitting alone in the abandoned union café, surrounded by a stack of magazines and waiting in vain. The pain of it all threatened to destroy him. It was too much for any one man to bear. His yearning for life became a disdain for it, and the only relief he wished for was death.

Since the beginning of human memory, cultures had tried to restrain this light with a name. Generations warned their children against its power and sought to grasp control by categorizing it to help their limited minds. Europeans called it Lucifer; the text of Isaiah said its name was the Morning Star; some on the continent of Africa whispered the name Mdyerekize; Haitians feared the dark dweller of the forests whose name was Grande Boi; the Cherokee knew its name to be *Kalona Ayeliski*, The Raven Mocker—the tormenter of the weak and the dying, that ate the heart of its victims. But none of these words taken together could ever fully capture the extent of this evil.

The Mocker defied all labels, just as it refuted the laws of physics that bound all other living things. It was a writhing orb that tore down the gift of life. It fed upon its own refuse, like a gathering of worms, consuming all within reach and re-birthing itself with disgusting energy. Found within was pride and envy, as well as the greed to take more, always more, than what one needed to the exclusion of all other life. There was madness and rage. And murder. The will to destroy life for no reason at all. It hated freedom, for that was the one reality that it could never have for itself, and that fact drove the false light to destroy all things of beauty that defied possession or ownership. It had waited here in its banishment, waited in this place of emptiness and stone, consuming itself. But here was a soul ready and torn, offering itself up in desperation; here was the broken soul that the Raven Mocker required.

Leonard found himself considering the imminent ruin of his life. He was persuaded by the deceptive promise of power that was set out before him, within reach. He decided this path would be superior to death. Within it, he perceived the guarantee of power, and much more strength than he could ever hold in his slight physique. Even his own father would fear him with such power. A strange line came to his mind, one that perhaps he had read or heard someplace long ago:

Given enough time, an ill spirit will find a willing vessel. And of what does an ill spirit enjoy in abundance, if not time?

Time. Time *was* what he needed; the answer was clear now. He simply had to have more time to get what he wanted. Len's mouth spread wide in a madman's grin, and so invited the light of the Raven Mocker to consume him.

Len dropped to the ground, and his muscles twitched in a violent seizure. Foam rose up through his throat and gathered thick and yellow around his mouth while his eyes rolled far back in their sockets, until nothing could be seen in them but white. The voice of a thousand legions forced itself through the foam in a language that had not been spoken aloud in generations. Leonard Harris was gone.

Chapter 12

Rachel and Shell

> *Said you'd give me light, but you never told me
> 'bout the fire.*
> Fleetwood Mac, "Sara"

After Major left camp, the Reese family sat around the fire with bowls full of untouched dinner. Each of them huddled with their private unrest. Rachel was hurt and angry with her father, but the dominant emotion she felt was fear. She feared the choice she had to make, even as Major sat out there in the woods, waiting. The hour in which the decision must be made drew nearer with every move the sun made toward the horizon. She did not fear walking out in the dark to meet Thomas at the ridge; the part she feared most was the decision she had to make when she arrived. She knew Major planned to leave for good.

There was a rustling in the nearby underbrush, outside the golden circle of light thrown around them by the campfire. Rachel wondered whether Major was out there. But she knew that he was not close; she felt the absence of him as sure as the absence of warmth when the sun disappeared behind a cloud. She pictured him now, out on the ridge, waiting. He would have built a small fire on the rocky outcropping, and would sit there, looking up at the sliver of a crescent moon.

Her vision of him shattered when an owl screamed. The first cry startled all of them. It was very close. The night pressed down and the surrounding forest seemed to come alive and close in against the fading light of the fire. The flames flickered as again the owl's call pierced the air. It came out of a tree directly beyond the boundary of the camp. They had heard many owls before, but this was louder than any of them, and its trill carried a haunting insistence. Without warning, another owl called out from the woods opposite the camp, as if in answer to the first.

This second response unleashed a hellish outbreak of call and response that reverberated in the air and did not relent for several minutes. The frantic exchange occupied all available space, and the very atoms surrounding them vibrated and threatened to explode. A shrill, high-pitched ringing pierced Rachel's mind, and she clapped her hands over her ears and hid her face in her chest. The sound itself was a living, dangerous being, and all three Reeses feared their eardrums might not withstand the enormous pressure rattling in their heads.

For the first time, in the wake of all that passed before their eyes since they had left Georgia, William Reese was frightened. No one moved. They sat cemented in place like beautifully painted statues with giant dark eyes. The owls stopped calling at the same time, and nothing more was heard for several minutes. The shrieking of the owls had terrified even the other forest creatures.

The dread did not belong to William alone, but had gripped the souls of Ani and Rachel as well. The owl's cry was a herald of death, all knew. The omen was an ancient one, passed down through generations as old as the Cherokees themselves. William's eyes closed, and he spoke to the sky as much as to his wife and daughter:

"You will both sleep in the wagon, and I will keep watch tonight. Let this bad medicine pass over us and return to the earth where it was born."

William pulled his rifle from the wagon. His weathered hands wrapped around the barrel, the skin over his knuckles stretching so tight that Rachel felt sure it would give way. She climbed on into the back of the wagon and pulled a worn quilt up to her chin. She could hear the sound of wet sticks breaking beneath her father's feet as he paced the perimeter of the camp.

Her mother settled in near the front of their wooden shelter, only six feet away. Soon her father took his watchman's place at the fire and became still. Rachel stared up at the crescent moon and wondered how long she would have to wait before he went to sleep.

The wait was much shorter than she could have dreamed, because not two full hours passed before the rhythmic breathing of her father's sleep reached her ears. He had fallen from a state of rigid alertness to a deep sleep, as though under the spell of some snake charmer's trance.

Rachel began to make her escape, not in steps but in millimeters. There would only be one chance to make her way out of camp without waking them. Her eyes darted downward to observe the movement of her left arm, from its position at her side to the top of the blanket. The timing of it was almost imperceptible, even to her. It required a stoic patience and a disciplined self-control that she had perfected in the houses of her playmates back home. Rachel would hide within feet of them and never be seen until just when she reached base and cried out, "Ollie, ollie, oxen, free!" They would turn and cry out in protest, certain she must have cheated somehow.

At this agonizingly slow pace, she thought it might take a full hour to be out from beneath the blankets, but by the time the covers were at her feet, the moon had scarcely shifted its cat's eye gleam upon her. She found herself standing at the wagon's edge and prepared to climb down the other side and disappear down the trail toward the ridge and Thomas Major.

She was struck by a terrible sadness as she stood there at the point of departure. Her father looked so vulnerable under the orange glow of the dying fire, his proud shoulders slumped forward. She saw that his grip had loosened on his rifle and that his hand lay across it in his lap. Though her mother was closer in distance, she could hardly make out her form in the darkness. She was covered in several blankets and lay with her back to Rachel. The edge of the blankets had been pulled up to protect the lower half of her face from the night air; this was the reason she was unable to hear Rachel's movement from her bed. Rachel felt a sudden compulsion to rush to her mother and hold on with all her might.

But she would not allow herself to betray Major. He was waiting, and the least she could do to honor their promise after all he had suffered was to go to him. The belief that she remained in his debt made her move against every instinct in her body. She was reminded of the dire cries of the two night owls, calling back and forth. Her memory of it was fresh, and it set alight some ancient part of her brain. It screamed out in protest that she must not leave the safety of her parents and the campfire. In one last desperate attempt to prevail, a shiver of terror ran straight down the length of her spine. Rachel froze with her hand on the edge of the wagon boards and waited for it to pass. Then she shook her head to discard the warnings, lifted her legs over the edge, and touched tiptoes silently to the soft earth below. Her mind went quiet as she slipped away into the dark to find Thomas Major.

※ ※ ※

While Major waited not more than a mile from the camp, he felt certain he knew what it must feel like to be stabbed in the chest. He almost wished himself dead. At least that vast nothing would quiet the tortured writhing in his gut and the screaming madness that gripped his brain. Little energy remained for an examination of how this end had befallen him. In his earlier retreat, the violent torrent in his mind had searched for a solution, but none came. The only feeling left was rage. Rage that brought the flicker of hundreds of images, each bearing another weight upon his soul: his father's silhouette as he rode off in to a blood red setting sun; the tears of his mother splashing down on his helpless hand while he sat in a chair at the side of her death bed; the sight of Rachel's slender figure vanishing in the night. The worst was the picture of the sick and starving children, whose skin hung sallow and loose from their shrinking bodies when he brought the medicine to the Cherokee camp. Mothers were reaching over the backs of the people who stood in front of them; they knew there was not enough to go around, but continued to beg, even while knowing that their babies would perish there in the cold. Children who would never know the warmth of a summer sun or the sight of a butterfly flicking its wings as it sat on a wildflower. Still, the women kept reaching; their arms appeared as tentacles, like some nightmarish sea creature alive in the crowded masses. Major did not have enough. He was not enough. He would never know their names. At last their faces faded away into the sky. Still, their dark, hungry eyes would never leave him. Instead, they populated his dreams every night, long after their bodies were placed in the ground.

To what entity did he owe this horror? In God's name, how was this evil allowed to exist? Major began to think that there was not just an absence of love in the universe but the persistence of a malevolent power that was allowed to appear at will to torture and mock its innocent victims. It must be a monster with bared incisors and terrible, oscillating eyes, set loose to take even the most innocent among them.

The thought of this evil began to cause his physical features to contort. There could be no satisfaction, no explanation, for the injustice, he thought. There was no hope.

Deep within the river valley, a sense of hopelessness and an energy of despair radiated out of Thomas Major and created a stir within the depths of the mud. The monster, as Major imagined it, had been exiled here, to exist away from the living in the deepest layers of silt and rock. This was its fate, this thing whose punishment for its deeds could be best understood in just one simple word: separation.

The light was the storm that drowned the weak, a falsehood that shone in the shadows of regret. It called out to the broken on their knees, to persuade them in its beauty that slavery was preferable to death. It was a voice of temporary comfort that whispered of a cheap salvation in the most desperate of hours. It was a manifestation of the sneaking thief that proclaimed that prosperity could only be found in its greedy ways. It held the promise of an instant remedy for pain. It was the night that swallowed the sun and ruined the world. The light was the most beautiful lie. *Kalona Ayeliski.* The Mocker.

There, upon the edge of the cliff, was the weeping man that would provide a vessel to destroy again. He was lost and alone, with no place to return to. The Mocker had waited there for thousands of years to find a vessel like this one to satisfy its existence. It was weak there in the wilderness, with nothing but simple animals to feed upon. The Mocker could not feed upon the willing; its ability to exist depended upon a weakened vessel, nearly devoid of will. Even so, the vessel must first accept its light. Given the proper circumstances, that part would be easy. The promise of sudden and great power, and the ability to control others, was an intoxicating offer that made for the safest of wagers among men. Still, this man who mourned and despaired on the cliffs above would soon destroy himself if the Mocker did not reach him, and then he would be of no use at all.

Thomas Major stood at the edge. He could just hear the rippling of the water below, though he was unable to see anything except the occasional silvery reflection of the crescent moon, winking with the river's movement. He had not bothered to look over the edge of the cliff earlier that morning, as he'd been in too much haste. At the time, he had only noticed the great expanse of sky that stretched out past the bluff. How was it possible that, even in his weakened physical state, just that morning—the very same day—he had been filled with such hope? How stupid and futile all of his efforts had been.

The sound of the water reached his ears again, and a strange thought came to him. He genuinely wondered how the river could continue to flow when his world was at its end. *God damn those clouds,* he thought, as he watched the wind push them in blackened groups across the sky. *Did not the world know it must stop in mourning?*

He curled his forearms up to his chest with his fists doubled up. "Why have you forsaken me?" he cried out loud, his voice echoing out across the valley and calling back to him, "*AKEN-ME, aken-me, aken-me.*"

Off in the far distance, a lone coyote answered with a solitary mournful howl. It gave him a sense of satisfaction that at least one other living being heard his cry.

He knew that Rachel would have come already if she wanted to leave with him. If she ever loved him at all. "Of course she didn't love you," he said out loud. He hardly recognized his own voice, bitter and desperate. *She used you like a fool.*

Major felt that his end was near, his days were done. He shuffled through the dark with the tip of his boot to locate the edge of the cliff. The only thing left was the jump. His boot found its mark less than six inches away. He realized that with only one step more he would have already fallen off the ridge accidentally. The thought struck his unraveled mind as hilarious, and he unleashed a roaring, mad laugh up at the moon.

He braced himself to jump, but just as his muscles tensed something caught his eye from far off down below. Though the sky had earlier been too dark to see by, there was now an unusual glow a few hundred yards down on the river bank. Even in his utter despair, Major was struck by curiosity. The light held a strange internal beauty. A glowing green tint seemed to be hidden deep within the thick fog gathered around it. Now Major noticed it was moving. It floated along the water's edge, rising and falling near the great boulders that flickered into view under its light.

Major felt a sudden urge to jump again. Not to kill himself now, but because he felt an overwhelming need to reach that light.

The insistence of the feeling consumed him, and he knew at once he could not go on without it. The light intensified as it approached, gathering in upon itself until it became a strong glowing orb of green light.

It travelled with ease up the face of the river cliff until it stopped directly in front of Major's face. It hesitated there, bathing the man in a pulsing illumination. His silhouette was visible in that moment for a mile in the distance. The entire sight, which lasted less than five seconds, appeared very much like the vibrant drawings that had been so carefully painted and pasted into ancient biblical texts a thousand years before.

The ascension of the Raven Mocker into the vessel of Thomas Major was not a frantic, violent scene, as had been depicted so many times before in texts and pictures concerning possession. Rather, the man stared for a moment into the blinding circle of light and saw a beckoning false promise—a promise of all the things he desired most. It was too much for his weak flesh to deny. In the end, Thomas Major did not only allow in the Mocker; he welcomed it.

※ ※ ※

As soon as she made it out of earshot, Rachel began to run. She could not sprint as she had the first time she ran to Major so many nights ago, but she made a steady pace through the forest, in the direction of the ridge. As she neared, she heard him call out, but could not make out the words. She ran faster now because she knew he would not risk waking her parents unless there was trouble. An unseen branch raked across her cheek as she ran. Blood came to the surface and made a line of truncated dots and dashes across her face. Rachel failed to register the pain. Her only concern was reaching Major. She could not imagine what might have happened to make him call out. Now came the sound of laughter, and it made her hair stand on end. That sound had no place out here.

She slowed and began to move with caution. Her mind screamed in terror that she must leave. *Turn*, it said. *Go back now; do not look back!*

But she knew she could not leave Major out there alone. He might be hurt. She finally reached a clearing, which opened from the road in a semi-circle, and stretched out to the great ridge over the river. Rachel thought, at first sight of Major, that this must surely be a terrible dream. She wished herself back under the warm covers, bundled in the safety of the wagon, her father at watch over them.

She wanted to wake up. But here was the sight of Major standing before her. Or at least it appeared to be him. His arms were drawn up so that his hands faced outward, his fingers held in a strange clawed configuration. The mouth that was once so full and graceful had now retracted into a crazed sneer, with part of his lip curled up to reveal a pointed canine tooth. The most frightening sight was the eerie green light that appeared to emanate from his mouth and lit the area all around him.

"THOMAS MAJOR!" She screamed, in hopes that it would shake him free of the evil that held him in its grip. "Thomas, what have you done?"

Even in the complete terror and confusion, she understood that something unnatural had happened here—nothing else could explain the change that brought this horror upon his face.

"What is it, darling?" he seethed. A hissing sound escaped from deep in his throat, and somehow he spoke with a lisp now that was never present before. Rachel heard a tinny, unnatural sound in his voice that was akin to the unnerving cry of a singing saw.

"My beautiful bride," he said. "My intended. Have you come to be with me at last?"

The body that once belonged to Major lurched forward and grabbed Rachel by her forearms with such an inhuman strength that it caused the small, bird-like bones of her forearms to snap in two. The moment she fell into his grasp, Rachel knew she would not survive. She began to pray.

"Yes, yes," Major cried. "Pray! Pray for salvation. Wait for an angel to ride down from above and carry you away! That is what you wished for all along, isn't it? To escape me?" He groaned when he spoke the words, as though a great internal struggle raged within.

"I was the one who saved the life of your grandmother," he said. "I left my life behind, trampled and forsaken in the mud of Tennessee, but none of that was worth your gratitude, was it?"

Rachel was quiet as a lamb at slaughter, so he shook her to get a response.

"Answer me!"

The light pulsed in his pupils, and he squeezed her broken arms again to get her to answer. She cried out in pain and made her last plea.

"Thomas," she said, "I know you are here; you can hear me. Rebuke this evil one and come back to me."

She moaned in agony, understanding death's proximity. The owls had come to tell her; they had come with the message that death was waiting right here on this cliff.

Major ignored her plea and began to drag her with him to the precipice. She went limp in his arms and focused the last of her will and energy—every thought—on rejoining Yowa. Major tightened his grip around Rachel's thin frame and lifted her up so that her face touched his. At long last, after all he had endured, she belonged to him, and that was all he needed. The last words she spoke pressed hot into the side of his face: "The light," she said. "Follow the light."

He did not have time to consider the great mystery that would live on in her words, because when the last had passed her trembling lips, he leaned over the edge with all the force of his weight and held fast to her. They tumbled off and fell in utter silence, except for the sound of the rushing wind protesting the union of their falling bodies.

❋ ❋ ❋

Ani was the one to find her daughter's body. All of the parties within earshot gathered the next morning to search the surrounding woods for Rachel. A few of them grumbled that this was the second time they'd been called upon to search for the Reeses's troublesome daughter; she was surely off on another mischievous ramble. They were certain she would return with an apology and offer up some childish excuse.

But William and Ani knew better. Their minds were black with fear. If only she *had* run away with Major. At least that would mean they might have a chance to see her again, alive, in this world.

Ani was able to forego her feelings of anger with William because of the panic that gripped her heart. They should have known Rachel would leave to go after that man. Of course she would; she loved him. Ani thought back to the time when she'd met William as a young girl; she would have done the same for him then. How easily the old forget the fiery passion of youth. But Ani had not spoken to William of his mistake. There was no need. He would never forget it himself.

They held out an impossible hope that Rachel might have wandered off and become lost. Perhaps they would find her curled up beneath a tree, and she would follow them back, sleepy eyed and regretful. But after a short time of calling her name and searching through the brush and in the caves along the river, Ani came to the outcropping not all that far from where they had slept. She saw in the dirt that two people had been there. She watched in quiet, helpless knowing as the footprints in the ground met and then danced to the edge of the rock. She steeled herself before peering off over the edge, because she knew the sight that waited below.

Rachel's body was in a tiny heap at the bottom of Devil's Promenade. Even after Ani screamed, no one touched her for a very long time. If they hadn't known better, they would have thought she was sleeping; her body appeared whole. Her long, dark hair floated out in a fan on the surface of the river, which flowed on just a few inches from the place where she'd fallen upon the rocks.

Beside her lay Thomas Major, his hand still clasped in a death grip around her wrist. The searchers turned their heads away from the grisly sight. After they'd fallen on the rocks below, some kind of an animal must have smelled a meal. Perhaps it had been one of the giant cats heard screaming near the camps late in the night. Whatever the predator had been, the onlookers whispered amongst themselves, it must have been something big, because a gaping, bloody hole had been left in the middle of Thomas Major's chest.

※ ※ ※

Shell stood there in the darkness for a good five minutes, without the slightest idea of what to do. Her cell phone was still in the truck, and even if it had been right here in her pocket, there would be no phone service this far out in the country. They hadn't passed a house for at least a couple of miles. There were many more cemeteries than homes, she had noticed, and she guessed that must be the situation for miles in the other direction too.

The worst part was that her glasses were in the truck. She was just about to go back for them when Leonard insisted that she sit down on his romance-pallet. Of all the times to lose her glasses, this was the worst. It was so dark out. Without her specs she was effectively blind. She felt lost and unsure, so she sat down on the blanket that now lay crumpled up at the side of the bridge. From here she could settle down, make a rational decision, and decide the best route.

At least Len had not remembered to take the flashlight in the midst of his fit, she thought, picking it up in her hand. She flicked the light off to save the battery. Overhead, a sudden breath of wind exhaled and coaxed the clouds to roll away from the jewel box of the sky. Shell looked up and welcomed the momentary respite from her predicament.

There, in the southeastern sky, stood Orion, the sober hunter regaled in full battle dress. At his feet awaited Canis Major and Minor, heralded by the brightest of all, the Dog Star Sirius. Shell imagined the two star dogs nipping at their master's heels in anticipation of quarry far across the galaxy. Directly north of Orion lay the Keyhole Nebula, offering its mysterious portal to whomever was lucky enough to bear the key to its lock. Now Rachel understood why she had never recognized the keyhole before; it was upside down in relation to Orion. She had read once that the width of the keyhole was a distance of seven light years. *Seven light years.* It was beyond contemplation.

Now that she was at last quieted by the constellations, the night sounds all around began to grow louder, or perhaps they had been the same all along, and she just had not noticed them during her excited exchange with Len. Fifty yards or so off the road, the sounds that ricocheted off the banks of a pond made an eerie evening lullaby. Frogs chirped their high-pitched sounds and their bigger bullfrog cousins joined in. They sounded like old men laughing back and forth over dirty jokes. Shell did not like the sound of it at all; it made her uneasy.

A bird call sounded off in the distance. It was a wild sound, not native to these parts; it sounded much like a monkey or a great ape. Fortunately, Shell had heard enough peacocks in her youth to recognize the noise. *Strange for pea fowl to be way out here*, she thought.

She heard the *yip, yip, yip* of a lone coyote. Then it was joined by several brothers. In no time, a seeming army of them joined to howl in unison. It was a terrifying sound, and for the first time Shell realized that she could be in real trouble out here, and no one would ever know or come to help. The coyotes continued their mournful song in the night, but now there was also a rumbling in the ground.

Shell's mind raced to fit all of these sounds within the confines of reason. If she could understand it, then she could dispel her fear. But she began to feel the first tendrils of panic curling into her brain like a morning fog rolling in, slow but sure.

The shaking ground was now accompanied by the clanking of heavy metal and screaming, howling coyotes. Shell imagined it to be the rabid cacophony of the dead. She pictured the dead digging out of the cemeteries that lined the road, raising back their skulls to howl along with the wild dogs, and clanging rotten bones against the iron stakes that fenced them in. Just when she thought the din could not get any louder, the whistle of a train sounded loud and lonesome as it passed by. The tracks must have been less than a half mile away, because the ground around her continued to shake. The train gave one last sad whistle as it rumbled off. Along with its departure went the cries of the coyotes and the croaking bullfrogs. All was silent now.

Shell's panic came on sudden and unexpected. Her heart pounded in her chest, and her eyes bulged out to pull in every possible point of light. Still, she could see nothing, especially not at a distance. She pinched her inner arm to settle herself down. It stung but did the trick; she felt the panic beginning to subside. That was an incredible comfort to her, for she knew that no sound decision could be made in a state of panicked chaos, and it was silly to give in to such things because of a train and a few vocal amphibians.

This is a situation you can handle, she assured herself. Now, she decided, was the time to act. Even if she had to walk all night, there had to be a house with a phone before too long. Two miles was nothing. She would take it slow, so as not to turn an ankle, and make her way toward some semblance of civilization.

She stood and flicked on the flashlight, flashing its meager tunnel of light down one way and then the other. She decided it was a toss-up. Might as well walk in the opposite direction than the one they drove in on. At least there was a chance she might pass by a farmhouse or something closer than the two-mile walk waiting in the other direction.

Shell took off walking, her converse sneakers crunching on the road with every step. She had not made any progress to speak of before she saw a light flicker dimly at the top of the hill off in the distance. It was fading in and out of view, and glittered a bit like a prism. Shell squinted into the night, blinking, knowing it was pointless without her glasses. She gave herself another mental kick in the rear for leaving them on the dash of the truck.

Well, yank my chain, she muttered. Perhaps she was meant to see the Spooklight after all. Several of the accounts she'd read online reported the light had this prism appearance, flashing mostly white but also blue and pink and green. She held her index and middle fingers at her temples and stretched her eyes out to try and pinhole a better glimpse of the light in the distance.

The light grew closer. Now Shell saw that there were two of them. She realized at last that they were the headlights of a vehicle. Her curiosity turned to relief. Out of the possible scenarios swirling in her head, she'd failed to imagine that some passing motorist might happen by on the road. She stepped off to the side in the ditch, just in case the driver turned out to be some drunk redneck out wheeling around in the country in the company of his truck and a case of beer.

Regardless of the person behind the wheel, she planned on flagging them down for a ride to the nearest phone. Drunk, or no. She still had the twenty in her pocket that Zeke had refused earlier; that would be enough to talk a ride out of anybody out here. *At the very least,* she thought, *it's enough to pay for another case of Natty Light.*

※ ※ ※

Len pressed his foot against the accelerator. *That silly bitch is still out here,* he said to himself at the sight of her outline up ahead. He nodded his head in anticipation. *Always waiting around for a fairy tale,* he thought. *Well, here comes Prince Charming.* The light emanating from his pupils surged with anticipation.

As he closed the short distance between them, he felt a driving sense of purpose and control for the first time in a very long time. He would show her now how wrong she had been; now the chickens were home to roost and it was Shell's turn to pay the price.

She was standing there, fingers at her temples, staring intently at the truck as it came into view. Her reaction was hilariously slow. At first she leaned forward, staring into his headlights. When the truck was in clear view, she snapped her spine back straight as a fence post. She stood there in shocked suspension, quite like a stunned animal, before a muscle in her body was able to move.

A sense of satisfaction spread through him. Len wanted her more now than he could ever recall before. The startled fear in her expression betrayed the illusion of the independent, strong woman she worked so hard to be. All in one honest moment, Len saw her innocence and vulnerability, right there on display. She was terrified of him now, and that made him hungry to see more.

※ ※ ※

By the time Shell realized the truck belonged to her father, and that Len was still at the wheel, it was too late to take cover. She was frozen in place for a moment. Her mind screamed, *Run, now! Get away!*

But Len had never so much as raised a hand in anger toward her. Besides that, where could she run to? And why give him the satisfaction of knowing she feared him now?

The truck bounced over several ruts in the road and skidded to a stop just a few feet away, the lights still beaming bright in her eyes. Len swung the door open and stepped out. His silhouette stood out against the darkened sky in the west. He was surrounded by a strange cloak of light. Shell had no time to consider its source, because in just two long strides he had a vice grip on her. His hands grasped both her upper arms just below her shoulders.

"What…What's happened to you, Len?" she spat. She was no longer able to mask her fear; there was no mistaking the rage displayed on his face. She was horrified by the stranger that looked back. It was almost as though Len did not recognize her. What stared back was the disaffected glare of a starving animal, taking in an eyeful of its first meal in weeks.

"Remember that old saying, Shell," Len spat. "'Three can keep a secret if two of them are dead?'" A snarl came to Len's lips. His throat was thick with mucous. He cleared it and spat the mess out on Shell's chest.

She realized then that the person she had long considered her friend, the one with whom she shared her bed, was gone. Len had lost his mind, and the hour for discussion had flown. Shell saw now that she would have to fight for her life.

Shell's immediate reaction was to use the move taught to her in self-defense classes. The first time she used it had been against little Jimmy White in the fourth grade. He had chased her across the playground all of recess, jerking at her ponytail. Eventually, Shell ran behind the play set and turned to face him. When he ran up and stopped, Shell popped her little knee right up into his crotch. She could still imagine the sight of Jimmy's pitiful face, leaned forward with his hands cupped over his zipper. His mouth pooched out in a grimaced "OH", before he dropped to the ground and lay on his side. His dramatic reaction had remained with Shell for all these years. It was a move that didn't require too much strength or technique. Since then a knee-in-the-crotch was, by her thinking, the equivalent of The Bomb.

She stopped struggling and pulled her foot back for extra leverage. She channeled the technique of her former nine-year-old self and shot her knee up between his legs. She landed the blow on her mark with a force that made her grit her own teeth. It was sure to drop Len, just as it had Jimmy.

But there he stood, unmoved. Leonard smiled back at Shell in a stunned look of disbelief. He picked her up while she fought and screamed, and carried her back to the truck. He easily subdued her with one hand and threw the door open with the other.

With a grunt, he tossed her into the cab and crawled in on top of her. There was no question what he had to do now. He had to squeeze the life from her. She had the nerve to try and fight back. Now she would finally understand that he had the control. In his hands lay the strength that could make her live or die. The last thought to pass through her mind would be the realization that she had no say over him anymore. He straddled her trunk and settled his weight squarely on top of her stomach so she couldn't buck him off.

She clamored desperately for any kind of leverage. The nails of her right hand broke off under the pressure as her fingers sank quick-deep into the flesh of Len's forearm. Crescent moons of blood began to rise from his pierced skin. A piece of gray vinyl peeled away from the dashboard in her clenched right hand. Shell's consciousness seemed to split in two. An internal voice screamed out in sheer terror. She found that some aspect of her being floated just above the struggle, looking down at the action below, like a calm and dispassionate observer. She was aware she could not last much longer, no matter how much she willed herself free.

With a sense of surreal incredulity, she became aware that in the midst of all the violence raining down, the playlist Len made for her was still playing from the speakers inside the cab.

Well, you're showin' me a different sign, Leon Russell sang in his sad, velvety voice, *even ask if the flame is dyin'. You'll get used to me baby...* An instant calm settled upon her when the unexpected melody floated in from the darkened heavens. She resigned to the beautiful and haunting lullaby. She was surprised by the relief washing through her mind at the prospect of allowing herself to release from the intolerable pain of death. Her body couldn't put up a fight anymore. Len was too strong.

A sudden river of blood gushed from Shell's nose and flowed backward into her eyes, which had begun to dilate. She felt, rather than heard, the slight popping sounds of blood vessels giving way in her eyes, too small and fragile to withstand any more pressure from the massive hands wrapped around her neck. Len's thumbs pressed down upon her windpipe with a crushing force. Leon's voice, that sincere and passionate plea for love, was the last sound to pass through her consciousness.

※ ※ ※

Once she stopped fighting, Len kept his hands at her throat for several more seconds, just to be certain he was done. He retreated from the cab, fishtailing backwards off of Shell's body and staggering away, woozy and high from the thrill of the kill. He grabbed the tailgate with both hands and allowed his head to hang down, suspended in the air. Rivulets of sweat ran down his forehead and stung his eyes with salt.

When his breaths slowed, Len climbed over the tailgate and sat down on the wheel well. He was surprised that now he did not feel very much at all. His body felt shot up with a heady opiate; he knew it was still there, but his mind had given up control.

A small voice from his conscience called out from the recesses of his mind, as if calling from the furthest room of an underground cave. It was a tiny, almost inaudible, voice, crying out for him to stop; that he had hurt her enough and now it was time to stop. But the light inside him drove him on; told him the thing he started must now be finished. He thought neither of the future or the past, and there was no longer a consideration for the woman he had once loved. He had no concept of empathy or sorrow for any of it. The good that once thrived within retreated, as a melting snowline at the advance of the first warm spring sun.

※ ※ ※

Shell was walking down a long dark hall. Someone came toward her. It was someone she knew and trusted. All of the fear was gone now. Yes, she knew this girl. This was her sister, her beloved playmate and confidante, Rachel. She smiled, but Rachel did not smile back. She was troubled.

"Let's go play!" Shell said, grasping her sister's hand in her own.

"You can't stay this time," Rachel told her.

Shell was confused. Of course she belonged here with her sister. They just had to pass through this dark place, and on the other side both of them would be free to run through the open fields in warm sunshine.

But Rachel turned to face Shell and stared deep into her dark eyes. Shell shook her head again to try and shake the fog from her mind. This wasn't Jennifer. How could this girl be her sister?

"Listen to me," said Rachel. "There is no time left for you here. I will wait for you to return, but for now you must wake up, my sister. The light. Follow the light."

※ ※ ※

Shell's eyelids fluttered. Her eyes felt like they were weighted down with bags of sand. At last she was able to force her left eye to part slightly—just enough to make out a strange shape in the darkness. For a moment, it was unclear where she was. An odd form slowly faded into focus from a blur. She began to see what looked like the outline of a tree, its sullen branches pointing at the ground, dead leaves swaying in the fickle breeze, resigned to falling.

She tried to raise her head. A sudden pain spread like a wildfire through her neck. She bit down hard to keep from crying out, and her front teeth pierced a crooked print into her soft bottom lip. Her head seemed to take on the weight of a cinderblock, and she didn't dare try and lift it again for a moment.

Somewhere just outside the cab hurried footsteps ground back and forth in the gravel. She was seized in an instant as the terror of Len's hands gripping her neck came flooding back into her muddied consciousness. For a split second, she tried to convince herself that it had only been a terrible nightmare; that she had dreamt the entire thing. But she knew there was no time for denial.

She decided for the moment to lie still and play dead. Maybe he'll just leave, she thought, her mind racing. Maybe he'll leave me here for dead, and after he's gone I can run for help. She lay there, eyes clamped shut, and strained to listen for a hint of what Len might be up to outside.

She could hear him humming a tune while he walked around the bed of the truck. There was the sound of him rummaging around, tools clanking against each other as he pushed them aside. Then came the strange sound of liquid sloshing inside a container. She was struck by a sudden desperate craving for water. She tried to lick her lips in an attempt to moisten them, even if only a drop, but her tongue was like a dry sponge raked across lips of sandpaper. She tried to swallow and couldn't. The sides of her tongue were grooved like the scalloped edges of a seashell. The sloshing sound outside made things worse, and she thought that just a single swallow of water would be the one source of strength she needed in order to get up and away. *Oh please God, please. Just one drop of water.*

She could hear Len rounding the back of the truck, the jug of liquid sloshing back and forth with each step as he drew closer.

※ ※ ※

Even as he sat in the back of the pickup, perched on the wheel well and staring down at a pair of Channellocks beside his feet, Len ground his teeth. He reached down and picked up the tool and held it out in front of his face. It reminded him of his father. That was what he would do, he thought. He could pull out her teeth and take them for a trophy.

He was certain Shell was already dead, but the fire inside him was not yet quenched. Hate and desire continued to consume him, and he felt he must satisfy it or perish with her in its flames. To see the life-light leave her eyes had not been enough. He would pull her teeth out the same way the bitch had pulled out his heart.

He bent over and scooped the tool up. It was cold and heavy in his hands. He bounced the Channellocks up and down in the air a couple of times, evaluating, thinking. Then his eyes darted over to the corner of the truck bed just behind the driver's seat. There sat a big red ten-gallon gas can. Ten gallons. That would do the trick. Ten gallons would burn every last ounce of her and dispose of the entire mess for good.

Shell's final trial by fire. Len found the play on words hilarious. He dropped the Channellocks back to the bed with a disinterested crash, then stood up and walked over to pick up the gas can, giggling like a hyena in the night.

When he tried to lift the can, he knew it was full, all the way to the top. *Oh, good ol' Dad, always prepared for emergencies, aren't we?*

This was the answer and the end, he thought. *Left to no one else but me.* Leonard picked up the gas can and dragged it to the edge of the truck bed. He hopped out and let the tailgate down, then pulled the gas can off the edge. It nearly dumped all over the ground; the petrol sloshed back and forth violently as Len steadied it with both hands.

"For better or worse, right, babe?" he said aloud.

When Len opened the door, the cab light came on and he stopped for a moment to take one last look at the woman that could have been his wife. She was still beautiful, he thought as he stared in, even with a couple of black eyes and a purple stripe in the shape of his own hands stamped around her neck.

He didn't take long to shake off the nostalgia. It was time to get down to business and get out of here. He lifted up the can and began to pour the gasoline all over her body and inside the cab.

※ ※ ※

The smell told Shell everything she needed to know about the liquid she heard sloshing in the container, before it ever touched her skin. Gasoline. Len was going to set her on fire. She knew that at any moment, in just a second, her skin would be in flames, and she would know how it felt to burn to death.

It seemed to take hours for Len to finish pouring out the fuel. In fact, he had only dumped out about half of the contents before he was satisfied. He felt certain that after a good fire started to burn, the gasoline tank would explode and finish the job for him. He rummaged around in the side pocket of the door for a lighter. He had noticed a Zippo down there earlier in the day. At last, his fingers closed around the metal rectangle. Within that tiny metal receptacle lay all he needed to finish the job. He appreciated the way it felt, cold and small against his palm. Then, using his thumb, he flipped the top open and held it out at arm's length so as not to catch himself on fire. *Safety first*, he thought.

It was the sound of the Zippo's hinged top flipping back that made Shell spring into action. All of the pain from the beating and the strangling was forgotten, pushed back into some other place for later retrieval.

Encapsulated here in this one moment, a final single second, was her last chance to survive. Shell felt a gathering of strength from reserves within her that she never knew existed. Strange words were echoing repeatedly in her ears and consciousness. *The light, go after the light.*

In one continuous, shocking spasm, Shell brought her knees up and kicked her feet at the Zippo's tiny flame that burned in Leonard's hand. In its illumination, she could see Len's face lit up from below. His appearance was ghoulish. She watched what happened next with a sort of disbelief and genuine amazement, as time slowed to a crawl and the action unfolded before her like a motion picture.

Her kick landed its mark all right, square on his left hand and the Zippo's flame. But she had also kicked past his hand and hit him in the chest. This caused him to stumble backward. In his shock, Leonard lifted his right hand to deflect the blow, but he was still holding the gas can and the petroleum splashed out directly into the Zippo's flame. A line of fire blazed up and followed the pouring liquid, all the way back up to the container. It exploded in his hand. Leonard was on fire.

The look that came to his face as he recognized what was happening mirrored that of little Jimmy White. It was a look of betrayal and disbelief, a gathering of the mouth in protest to emit that unfortunate, grimaced, "OH," before he dropped to the ground. He rolled around in the rocks to try and extinguish the flames that consumed him.

Shell didn't waste a second. Time sped up as though to catch back up with the present. She was still soaked in gasoline, along with the cab, and she knew that if Len got up and reached the cab, they would both burn. She sat up and slammed the driver's door shut with her left hand, then turned the key that was blessedly still in the ignition with her right. The truck started up and she jerked the gear shift into reverse and hit the accelerator.

The truck lurched backward, but after it moved just a few feet, the right rear tire lifted up the entire frame and rolled right on over something in the road. Shell thought at first it must have been the basket Len left out on the road. But no, she realized, it was not been a basket. The wheels of the truck had been lifted by something much larger. Something much more substantial.

Shell slowly fit the puzzle pieces together one by one: *Len set on fire. On the ground. Under the truck.* At last the full picture emerged and formed a cohesive picture of what she had done. In his panic to extinguish the flames, Len rolled beneath the truck and she had run him over. It was a horror too immense to grasp. Shell was in shock now, and the subconscious part of her mind that concerned itself with survival alone took over again. The truck turned around in the middle of the road and headed back in the direction of home, though Shell would not remember that part. She never looked back at the burning body in the rearview.

Chapter 13

Shell

> *We could just start over, but it's oh so hard to do, when you're lost in a masquerade.*
> Leon Russell, "This Masquerade"

Shell had no idea how she managed to make it back home. She sat in the driveway slumped over the steering wheel unable to move. Her head was a pounding mass of surreal images she could not push away. She was shaking and cold. Her clothes and the entire cab were soaked with gasoline. Even her hair hung limp and greasy, drenched through with gasoline.

The sun was coming up. *But how can that be,* she thought. *How could it be morning? Hadn't it been just after midnight when Len stopped on Spooklight Road?*

The thought of his name brought the grisly scene rushing back to her like a rogue wave, crashing and dragging her down into the swirling undertow of chaos. She could not accept that Len had tried to kill her. Had it been a nightmare? She wished it so, but knew by the stinging sensation in her nose and the whining in her ears that this was very much her new reality. It was a nightmarish one that even the most depraved of horror films could not have conjured up.

She knew there would be safety inside her parents' house. If she could only will herself to move in the direction of that door. It was the front door she had pushed her way through so many thousands of times, never questioning the safety on the other side. That was the thing she desired most right now—a feeling of security that had been left on a scant dirt road way out in the farthest corner of Oklahoma. *It might never be found again*, she thought.

Then the sound of the front door reached her ears. Her father rose each morning with the sun, and she knew it would not be long until he found her there in the cab of the truck. But after a few seconds, the voice that sounded in alarm was not Dean's but Christie's. Shell heard the sound of her mother's house slippers shuffling across the gravel drive, and, for the first time in eight hours, Shell knew that she would live.

The driver's side door of the truck swung open and Shell slumped out, her mother's body propping her up before she could fall to the ground.

"Oh my God, Shell, what happened?" She screamed as she took in her daughter's wasted visage. "Dean!" Christie yelled at the house. "Dean, get out here now! It's Shell!"

Shell closed her eyes.

"How long have you been out here," Christie demanded. "Where is Leonard?"

Shell could not find the energy or will to answer her mother's questions, but slung her arm over her shoulder. She used the hood of the truck to help bear her weight until Dean came out to the porch. He stood there a moment, watching in disbelief with a mug of coffee in his hand, until Christie shattered his daze.

"Get over here and help me; she's hurt!"

Dean snapped to action and sprinted the short distance to Shell and Christie, his bare feet glancing over the sharp rocks and gravel. He put his arm around his daughter's waist, and together he and Christie pulled her across the forty yards to the front porch.

"Go wake up Jennifer," Christie said, "and tell her Shell needs a change of clothes. And bring a pan of warm water."

Christie's tone had switched from sheer panic to business, and she set about the task of reviving Shell. After they carefully set her down in a patio chair, Dean raced back indoors to wake Jennifer. Christie began to peel off Shell's gasoline-soaked clothes. They had dried and stuck to her skin in places along her legs, and Shell's limp body jerked like a marionette each time her mother tugged.

Jennifer came stumbling outside, rubbing her eyes, annoyed at the commotion outside. In her hands she held a pair of gym shorts and a worn old army T-shirt. Christie reached over and snatched them from her grasp while Jennifer stood motionless and stared at her sister, who appeared to be some otherworldly refugee. She was hardly recognizable.

Once they got Shell changed into the clean clothes, Christie told Jennifer to take the fuel-soaked clothes behind the house to the burn barrel.

Dean was back outside now, so they helped Shell inside to the bed. Shell had not managed a word of explanation, but she motioned to her mouth and Christie knew she was in desperate need of water. She fetched a bottle from the kitchen and administered it to her daughter in small sips. Shell thought the cool precious liquid tasted better than anything else in the world.

Her head lolled back on the pillow and she blacked out, those bursts of fireworks exploding across the backdrops of her eyelids again. She felt her sister's gentle hand on her shoulder, and she returned back to consciousness.

"Sister, you're going to have to stay awake just for a little while." Jennifer instructed. "You have to tell us a few things about what happened and then you can rest."

Shell's eyes rolled around like marbles in a jar. They were beyond the control of her own will, and in their movement she picked up on the contorted and worried faces of Dean and Jenny looming behind her mother's.

"Len's dead." She managed to whisper.

Her mother's hand shot up to capture the gasp that escaped her mouth.

"It can't be! Tell us where he is, Shell, and we'll call the police. You have to wake yourself up now; he might still be alive and need help."

Shell reached deep within herself for the last of her strength and closed her eyes. She began to relate the terrible events as best she could.

"We went out to look for the light." Her breaths came in short, raspy mouthfuls, and she had to pause at great length between each sentence. Her family stood at the bedside, riveted and terrified at each word.

"We had a flat and had to get help from a man—a man at the side of the road. He knew... he warned us not to go." She blinked up at the ceiling as though she might find an answer up there in its universe of drywall ridges. "I thought we were coming back here, but Len decided to go after the Spooklight.

"When we got there, we had an argument. He left with the truck...left me by myself out there." Her chest hitched at the thought of that darkness and the memory of what had emerged for her out of it.

"When he came back," she said, "he was...he was different. Leonard tried to kill me." She raised her head and shoulders up off the bed in a flurry of movement, and her mother's hands gently forced them back down again.

Her hands went to her neck and felt the impression of where his hands had been.

"He poured gasoline over me and tried to set me on fire."

"That sonofabitch!" Jenny cried. "I knew it! I knew something was wrong with him!"

Dean Foster silenced Jenny with his hand on her shoulder.

"It wasn't him," Shell continued. "It wasn't Len. Something happened to him. He lost his mind."

"What happened next, Shell?" Christie coaxed her to continue.

"I woke up. I blacked out. Maybe I died, but an angel told me I had to come back. I still don't remember why she made me come back."

Her family exchanged uneasy glances. Shell was still in a severe state of shock. Her mother pulled the blankets up to her chin.

"Just tell us where he is, Shell." Christie said. "You're safe now; he can't hurt you here. But we have to send someone out to try and help him. You have to tell us where he is."

"He's dead in the road." Shell said flatly, emotionless. "He caught on fire. I ran him over. I felt the wheels go over his body."

The three of them strained at her words, certain they had not heard correctly.

"Did you say 'fire'?" Dean asked, but his voice was far away, Shell imagined he was at the end of a long hallway back at her elementary school, shouting the echoing words across a great distance. With that last conscious thought, Shell's mind took control and put her into a sleep that none of the family was able to interrupt. Over the course of four hours, her thoughts retreated into a dark nothingness wherein no horrors could touch her molested mind.

The family left her alone, except to go in and monitor her breathing every few minutes. They knew she had endured a terrible trauma. Even if her description of the events was inexact, something awful had clearly happened. Dean suggested she might be under the influence of some kind of hallucinogen; that she might have imagined the entire story. But none of them believed it, even if they wished it so.

Christie called the highway patrol and reported Len missing. She gave his description as best she could remember; including the clothes he wore when he left the day before. She told them she had reason to believe he was hurt badly on one of the dirt roads up around Quapaw, somewhere around Spooklight Road.

She gave them her name and address, but left her daughter's name out of the report. After all the untold horrors Shell had lived through, she could not endure an interview with the police just yet. When she recovered, they would take her up to headquarters, and she would tell them everything she remembered.

Dean had gone out behind the house and lit the clothes in the burn barrel on fire. Christie dispelled the notion that he should drive up to Ottawa County and drive the back roads looking for Len. He felt relieved that she said no. In truth, Dean thought that if he had found Len, and he was still alive, he would be hard-pressed to keep from finishing off the job, if the story Shell told him turned out to be true. He was beside himself with unanswered questions and despair for his disfigured daughter. The sight of her was akin to a Halloween mask. He had been forced to turn away from her gaze, for she had blood in her eyes. Not a speck of white remained to be seen in them.

Jenny went back in to sit at her sister's bedside, watching Shell's slow respirations come and go. Several times, when the breath escaped Shell's lungs and too much time passed before her chest rose again, Jenny felt on the cusp of dialing 911. But Shell kept breathing, and her pulse was stable now. There was nothing for them to do but wait. After she watched for over an hour and was sure Shell would not die there in her bed, Jennifer returned to the living room and joined her parents. They were sitting there side by side, speaking in low whispers, each holding a cup of coffee without even a sip missing. They stared at each other, united in helplessness and fear.

Jenny sat down on the love seat opposite them and curled her legs beneath her body. Hardly a word was spoken until they heard the soft scuffle of feet in the hall.

Shell emerged in the room and appeared lost, looking at her surroundings to gather herself.

"How did I get here?" she asked. "Where's Len?"

No one could provide an answer for, in truth, they did not know. She stood there staring at them, a disheveled specter, made humorous by the topknot that sat flush on the top of her head, tied by Christie.

Shell's legs were weak and trembling. She decided to make for the couch to sit down, but before she was able to take the first step, a loud knock sounded at the door.

She froze in place, her eyes wide with fright. Her mind was a blank slate and she was void of memory, but instinct and the force of the fist upon the door brought her heart to a full stop.

"Oh jeez," Jennifer said. She was turned in her chair, looking out the front window. "It's the cops."

SHELL

Any other day, and on many occasions before, the phrase would have evoked a round of laughter. But for now the laughter was gone. and none of them could have guessed how much time would pass before they might enjoy that simple luxury again.

Dean walked to the door and opened it, standing tall and brave in the doorway. Three highway patrolmen stood just outside in full uniform, weapons in hand.

"Mr. Foster?" the officer asked Dean in a commanding voice.

"That's right," Dean replied. "I'm Dean Foster."

"Where is your daughter?"

"Which one?" he said, tight-lipped.

The officer peered in over Dean's shoulder and saw Shell standing there, still frozen in place.

"There she is," he said, pushing Dean aside. Dean attempted to push back, and two of the officers took him to the ground with a baton across his back.

Christie screamed and cried out, "No, no, please don't!"

The officer who knocked on the door ignored her cries and grabbed Shell by the shoulder. She was whisked around and found herself staring back down the long hall to the bedrooms. She heard the metal clicking sounds and felt the tight pinch of the cuffs as they snapped together around her wrists.

"Shell Georgene Foster, you're under arrest for the murder of Leonard Harris."

The rest was a blur as Shell was whisked out of the house and propelled toward one of the waiting patrol cars. She saw out of the corner of her eye that one of the officers was walking behind the house to inspect the burn barrel.

The arresting officer opened the rear door and pushed her head down into the backseat cage. Even after the door was secured, she could still hear Christie's helpless cries from the porch. Dean was continuing to argue with the officers, but he was subdued now by the overwhelming presence of the third officer, who had returned to assist in silencing his protests.

Shell sat spent and numb, oblivious to the impossible scene unfolding all around. At last the officers returned to the two patrol cars and began to drive away. The only relief she held on to was the grateful realization that the other two officers had not arrested her father too.

Jennifer ran up to the window and screamed at her sister through the glass. Her face was covered in red welts, and her face glistened in the sun.

"Shell!" she cried out. The tiny blue veins at her temple stood out in distress. "We know you didn't do it, and we're going to get you back!" Her voice trailed off as she fell behind and the cruiser's speed accelerated down the driveway.

Shell blinked and watched the colors speed past the blackened window frame all in a blur. The rusted-steel parallel lines of a barbed wire fence raced past. At the onset of summer, the dark tangle of briars would be covered with delicate white blooms, and later they would hang low with sweet purple blackberries. A tiny red cardinal sat in the crook of the old oak tree that stretched the fractal miracle of its branches up toward the slate gray sky.

The beauty of the world outside came over Shell in wave after wave of emotion and she was overcome. A tiny drop of water fell upon her cheek and tracked its crooked path down toward her chin. Then, like a flood, the rest followed the first in a trail of tears that had waited there dormant for so long.

> *Did not you know, when you hurt me so cruelly,*
> *I was your love, I was your friend.*
> *You couldn't stand that I was so free;*
> *now you will never see me again.*
> Levon Helm, "Golden Bird"

Bibliography

Dale, Edward Everett. *Cherokee Cavaliers.* University of Oklahoma Press, Norman. 1939.

Foreman, Grant. *Indian Removal.* University of Oklahoma Press, Norman. 1932.

Mooney, James. *Myths of the Cherokee.* Dover Publications, New York. 1995.

Made in the USA
Middletown, DE
10 June 2022